The Adventures of Captain Chase Sykes & Navigator Duncan Sampson

Shayne Carmichael and Mychael Black

Published by Arian Derwydd Books, LLC, 2024.

A campy scifi comedy/romance from the minds of Black and Carmichael. Giant assassin vampire sheep, a secretive jungle lord, saving the universe, and screwing each other are all a part of the every day life of Chase Sykes and Duncan Sampson. Galactic Interferion's best men are at the forefront of all the action, living and lovin' large. Chaotic Insecure threatens the stability of the known universe in his plot to steal Interferion seeding crystals. But all is not right in Duncan and Chase's world, and they wonder if they're working for the right side.

Interferion Universal Date 98275615957435652-1 Log-Duncan Sampson/Message to Dad.

Dad,

I swear everything is fine. I know you've heard the news, but relax. I'm not one of Interferion's Most Wanted anymore. It's a long story, and half the time, I'm still not sure of everything that happened. Most of it seems like a blur.

How in the hell did we get caught in the middle of the machinations of a power hungry madman? Okay, I can't regret a moment of it. It brought Eezy into our lives. Until we met him, Duncan and I were content to float along the cosmic waves, only too happy to fuck whatever gorgeous creature who happened to come our way.

No, you don't have to say it; I was even worse before I met Chase. Chase was the one that taught me I could rely on him always being there. Everyone else came and went, but it would always be the two of us in the end no matter what. Why in the hell do you think I married him?

I know you weren't too happy that Chase isn't a royal, and I really appreciate that you've said little about my choice of a husband. I'm even more appreciative you've kept mom from interfering. Does she even know you sent the Eala royal tioya as a wedding present? I promise I won't say a word about it.

Now, a bit about Eezy. Eezy is the one who has settled us the most. You're not going to believe this, but neither Chase nor I even batted a lash when we escorted Ivernon to Alpar-12. The universe's most famous actor, and Chase and I didn't even try to get into his pants. You can pick yourself up from the floor now, Dad. I swear it's true.

You'll have a chance to see for yourself when we all visit. I've been begging Arch for some time off, and he promised we'd get some by the end of the year.

You know I've always been happy working with Interferion. Couldn't have a better boss than Arch. It wasn't until he dragged me out of that Hebernia bar and slapped a uniform on me that I found any kind of purpose. Yes, you wanted me to rule Eala, but you know damn well Aaron is better suited than I am to do that. My brother makes a lot better ruler than I would have.

I'm rambling, and you'll want me to get straight to the point. Knowing you'll want all the facts about everything that happened, I'll try to tell you everything that went on. You can pretty much figure the universal news casts had it wrong. Chase and I aren't traitors. Arch has been trying to do damage control, but the full facts haven't been released yet.

You've heard of Rudolpho, the underground trader, right? Well, Chase and I were doing our usual supply acquisition from him when it all started...

Episode One: In the Future?

Chapter One

Six months earlier...

"Release the giant assassin vampire sheep!" Rudolpho screamed out the command. In answer, the portal opened and dozens of hungry sheep streamed into the room.

Duncan gazed in wide-eyed horror as he clung to the swinging iron chain above the warehouse floor. His partner, Chase, stood directly in the path of the oncoming sheep—but then, so did Rudolpho.

"Chase!" Duncan yelled before the ravening flock engulfed their arch nemesis. Rudolpho's piercing screams echoed in the warehouse and Chase glanced upward. He tried to reach for Duncan's leg as Duncan swung toward him.

"Let go and I'll catch you! Hurry!" Chase's gaze darted back and forth between Duncan and the mass of wool.

"I'll get you for this!" Rudolpho's vengeful vow came from the bottom of the pile. "Nerk, you incompetent..." The bleating of the sheep drowned out Rudolpho.

After Duncan freed himself from the chain using his All Purpose Metallurgic Dissolver, he jumped into Chase's waiting arms, muttering, "Thank God for Nerk."

Once Chase set him on his feet, they both ran from the warehouse, leaving Rudolpho to the revenge of the sheep.

Chase raced to the ship that sat just outside the warehouse, flipping open the voice pad in his hand. "Mal, get 'er running!"

"Yes, Captain Sykes," the computer voice answered.

Once inside, Duncan collapsed into his chair before gales of laughter erupted. "Did you see Rudolpho's face? I think we need to hire Nerk. Opening the portal right in front of Rudolpho? Absolutely priceless."

Chase grinned and spun around in his chair, leaving Mal to get the ship off the ground. "We really should," he said, relaxing back in the chair. "So, did you get the converter?"

"Nerk does more to defeat Rudolpho than we do." Slipping his hand inside his regulation Galactic Interferion jacket, Duncan pulled out the gleaming silver rod and waved it triumphantly in front of Chase's face. "Told you I could."

Sticking his tongue out, Chase snatched the rod from Duncan's hand. "Showoff. Oh, this one's nice. Heavy. How much is it worth again? Twelve hundred creds, isn't it?"

The station com screen flickered and the face of Arch, Interferion's coordinator, appeared. Hastily Duncan grabbed the converter and hid it before it could be seen.

"Chaotic Insecure is on the move. Quadrant Delta, Vector Z. You've got two microns to get there." Arch's gaze darted between Chase and Duncan. "And I saw that. It had better be on my desk when you return from your mission."

"Damn," Chase muttered. "Yes, sir. Roger that. Sykes and Sampson out. Two microns. Ya know, that gives us ample time for some action," he said, wiggling his eyebrows at Duncan. He leaned forward and hit the button to switch off the screen.

"Go away, Arch, we're busy." Rolling his eyes, Duncan covered the view bot with his hand and motioned to Chase with the other. Even though Chase had turned it off, Duncan didn't trust it. "Over here in my lap, babe. We've got two microns to kill."

A few of Arch's more choice expletives filled the cabin before the sound was abruptly cut off.

Chase grinned and stood, stripping before straddling Duncan's lap. "Mm," he hummed. "Hey, babe. You know, you really looked good hanging from that chain…"

Satisfied Arch was gone, Duncan rested his hands against Chase's hips as his lover settled on his lap. "I didn't miss your hard on. It was the sheep, wasn't it?" Snickering, his nails grazed over bare skin as he tipped his head back, looking up at Chase.

"Smart ass," Chase mumbled, mouth moving over Duncan's. "Although, they might make a good set of sheets." He rocked over Duncan's lap, groaning softly.

Nipping at Chase's lower lip, Duncan tugged gently before releasing it to remove his jacket and shirt. One of his hands lowered between them, closing around Chase's cock. Turning his head, he whispered in Chase's ear, "Two microns gives me just enough time to bury myself in your ass."

Chase nodded emphatically, gasping. "Slick," he panted, groping blindly around the console. "Need something slick…"

The pressure of Duncan's fingers engulfed Chase's cock in a slow rhythm, deliberately increasing the need of his lover's body. Since he couldn't get up to take his pants off just yet, Duncan remain where he was, content to play.

"Yes!" Chase crowed, finally coming up with a half-empty tube of some off-brand lube. He dropped a quick kiss to Duncan's lips and slid off his navigator's lap. "Come on, baby," he said, popping open the tube, "lemme ride that sweet prick."

"We better stop and buy some more." Chuckling, Duncan stood and stripped off his pants. He stroked his cock lazily as he grabbed the lube from Chase. Then he settled back into his chair. Drizzling a thin film of gel over his rigid flesh, he glanced up at Chase.

Chase licked his lips and nodded as he straddled Duncan again, groaning as he slid down onto Duncan's cock. "Oh, yeah." He captured Duncan's mouth with his, wiggling his hips to settle Duncan deeper inside him as he plundered the navigator's mouth with his tongue. With a muffled groan, Duncan thrust up and buried his cock deep in Chase's ass. His mouth tightened around Chase's tongue and he scraped his teeth over it. His life partner never failed to excite the primal need in one hell of a rush over Duncan's senses.

Hands tight on Duncan's shoulders, Chase rode him hard, sliding and grinding and bucking, hips working overtime. Letting go, Chase pushed a hand between them, wrapping it around his cock.

"Come on, baby," Chase panted, working his fist up and down as he bounced on his lover's lap, "make me come, D."

Growling with the exertion, Duncan slammed hard and deep into Chase. His hand took over as it pushed Chase's away and the tight circle of his fingers ran along his lover's cock. His thumb pressed and rubbed against the sensitive slit as shudders began to roll through his own body. Panting heavily, Duncan's head fell back against the head rest with a thud and with a sharp yell, he came.

"Oh, fuck yes!" Chase jerked and bucked, come spilling over Duncan's fist. Collapsing onto Duncan's chest, Chase panted and gasped, working to catch his breath. Just as he opened his mouth to say something, the sound of a throat clearing stopped him cold.

"If you two are done," Arch said from the screen, "I thought you might like to know that you'll have backup for the Chaotic Insecure job."

"Christ in a hand basket, Arch. Must you eavesdrop?" Ignoring his boss, Duncan slid an arm around Chase, holding him quietly as he smoothed his hand against Chase's hair.

"Do you blame me?" Arch gave them both a wry grin. "I've already fed the coordinates into your ship. Your back up will be waiting. Have fun, boys." With that, the screen flickered to black.

"He has a bad habit of overriding the system," Chase muttered. "Remind me to fix that shit when we hit port."

"Remind me to smack him upside the head when we return to base," Duncan grumbled as he buried his face in Chase's hair.

Mercifully the voice com remained silent this time.

Chase nodded, humming as he slid his arms around Duncan's neck. "Should be reaching the—"

Mal's metallic, synthesized drone cut him off. "Delta Quadrant, Vector Z within range, Captain Sykes."

Sighing, Chase kissed Duncan and stood slowly. "Thank you, Mal."

"Should make Arch save the damn place this time." As Duncan stood, he pressed a small blue button on the console. A barrier of molecules circled around them as the tube came down before a spray of water hosed over their bodies. A second later, a blast of warm air dried them. Then the barrier faded.

Chase chuckled as he dressed. "That'll be the day."

After putting his clothes back on, Duncan leaned over the navigation screen. "Where in the hell did Arch send us anyway?" Pressing the screen, he saw the planet they were approaching. "Iceu. Who in the hell are we picking up from Iceu?" Duncan settled back in his chair, strapping himself in for the descent to the planet.

"Iceu..." Chase mulled it over as he buckled in. "Bloody hell," he grumbled as he took Mal off pilot duty. "Watts and Myers are on Iceu."

Duncan turned on the viewing screen. A vast forest sprawled beneath them as the ship passed through the planet's upper atmospheric level. There were no cities on Iceu. Only small villages and isolated posts dotted the heavily-wooded planet. Iceu had one undisputed ruler, and Iari allowed very few outside people on his world.

"I still wonder how Arch bribed Iari to have a Galactic post on this place."

It'd been a subject of much speculation and merriment among the GI crews. Arch had been the only one to meet with Iari during the negotiations, so naturally imaginations ran wild.

Chase snorted as he took the ship down toward the landing pad. "Like that isn't obvious," he chuckled. He eased the ship down, letting the thrusters settle it nice and gentle. A few minutes later, the ramp opened and Chase unbuckled and stood. "Well, might as well see what Arch and the boys have for us tonight."

Unfastening the belt, Duncan stood and waited for Chase to lead the way. Eyeing his lover's back, he murmured, "If anybody fires, it hits you first."

"I'm skinnier and quicker," Chase shot back, "so I can dodge it." He gave Duncan a wink before grabbing his holster and strapping it around his waist. He double-checked the quadblaster, ensured it was set to snare only, and started down the ramp.

Chapter Two

Snickering, Duncan followed behind Chase, crossing the pad to the outpost door. The small building looked completely deceptive in size. Roughly forty by forty feet, it only held a few offices of the quadrant staff and the elevator that led to the underground base. As they stepped inside, a blast of cool air hit them from the building's cooling system. Not even bothering with the fourth level clerk, they brushed past her desk, heading toward the office of the post commander.

"Well, hello to you, too," she called out sarcastically.

"Sorry, Lenra," Chase tossed over his shoulder, "but we're still on-duty."

Duncan didn't bother to knock on the commander's door. As he opened it, Virl Talin stood from behind his enormous desk.

"Ten years and you still haven't learned to knock?"

"You weren't expecting us?" Duncan shrugged before he added as an afterthought, "Sir."

Watts and Myers stood near the commander, smirking at them. Another man, neither Duncan nor Chase had ever seen, stood near the rear open door of the office.

Commander Talin just sighed. "I wouldn't tolerate you two," he grunted as he sat back down, "but you're the best we've got."

"Okay, so what've you got for us, sir?" Chase asked as he collapsed into the nearest chair. He didn't even give Watts and Myers the benefit of a nod. The other man, though... now that one he did notice. And if the look on Duncan's face was any indication, Duncan noticed him, too.

"Your Highness, this is Duncan Sampson and Chase Sykes, two of Interferion's best." Looking over at them, the commander continued, "And this is Iari, Ruler of Iceu."

After they'd been introduced, Duncan cast an appraising gaze over Iari. Both of them had heard of the secretive jungle lord. In person, his blood-red hair made him a temptation worth grabbing. His high cheekbones gave him an exotic appearance guaranteed to appeal to anyone with a heartbeat. A deep red tunic ended right at his upper thigh, giving them a tasty glimpse of the mouth-watering cock underneath. Reflective umber eyes fastened on both of them.

With a regal nod, Iari greeted them. "I will be accompanying you both to deal with CI. I have fought him before."

Duncan arched a brow, murmuring, "We must be on Arch's 'I Love You' list."

Chase was too busy just staring. "Yeah."

"Captain Sykes," Commander Talin said sharply, "is our best pilot. Sampson is his navigator."

"Among other things," Chase added with a thoroughly lascivious grin. Talin groaned.

The smile on Iari's lips matched the amusement in his eyes. "We should head to your ship and discuss our plans."

As to what those plans included, Iari didn't say, but the element of interest in the gaze fastened on the two of them gave Duncan more than a little hope. This would be one hell of an interesting adventure.

Chase resisted the urge to lick his lips. He stood and moved back to Duncan. Hand on the door frame, he leaned over slightly and whispered, "Remind me to thank Arch profusely for this."

Iari walked over to the door, seemingly oblivious that his tunic rode up just enough to show everything. Judging by the lack of regard for his under-dressed state, it was clear that Iceu's clothing-optional policy still remained blessedly intact. Equally clear was the hard-on Duncan now sported. His gaze followed Iari as the king moved out the door.

The commander's voice sharply intruded on their lust-filled thoughts. "Captain Sykes, CI must be stopped before he reaches Pegdar. The planet has already been seeded by the Galactic AG sens-a-trons. Watts and Myers will be with you on this mission as well."

"Shit." Chase nodded and waved nonchalantly, shouting over his shoulder, "Watts! Myers! Get your butts in gear and on the ship. Now!"

"Yes, Captain," Myers answered wryly.

Iari chuckled softly as Chase passed him and he followed behind. Duncan followed behind Iari, completely content with the view afforded by the short tunic. The outfit was a poor cover for the man's muscular rear. Especially since each movement hiked the material high enough to expose a good half of his ass.

As they boarded the ship, Duncan motioned to Myers and Watts. "Stow your gear, guys, and buckle up for Hydra." Moving past them, he very courteously helped Iari into one of the chairs on the captain's deck

Stepping to the console, Duncan leaned over slightly, turning on the Dimensional Cosmodoodler. Viewing the scan screen, he noticed the lack of humanoid life on Pegdar. "Looks like Talin already had the AG teams evacuated. I'd say the man lacks faith in our skills, Chase."

Iari relaxed back into the seat and rested his chin on the tips of his fingers, simply watching.

"More like he knows us well enough to get them the hell out of the way," Chase said as he buckled in. Hitting a button on the console, he said into the com, "Buckle up, boys! We gotta make star tracks."

As soon as Duncan was settled and belted in, Chase took the ship up and made a straight shot out of the Iceu atmosphere. The clouds disappeared, fading into the void of space and lights of the stars.

Once on course, Duncan signaled Chase with a wink and a look in Iari's direction. Watts and Myers were on the back deck, ignoring everybody else.

Murmuring in a low voice, Duncan said to Chase, "As soon as we're done and we've ditched the Hardy Har Har twins, we oughta take His Highness to the Ionesphere."

Chase glanced discreetly in the ruler's direction. "We'll need to make a stop at the Farliff Port. I'll be damned if I'm going anywhere without more lube."

"There is a smaller port just outside of the Ionesphere," Iari chimed in quietly. "The oils there are exquisite."

Duncan's lips twitched in a smile. "He's right."

"Pegdar in range, Captain," Mal's voice interrupted them and the view screen turned on, showing the heavily-clouded mass of the planet.

Duncan pulled down the scan screen and checked the planet's surface. "Still no humanoid life forms on the planet. Looks like we arrived before CI."

"Gives us time to set up." Chase took the ship down, keeping a close watch on the scanners. "All clear." Pressing the com, he announced, "We beat CI, but there's no guarantee on time. Suit up!"

Activating the secondhand nuclear-powered Oglernoid, Duncan cloaked the ship as it dipped down into the misty atmosphere of Pegdar. "Silence lock down, starting now. Tel-com only."

"We battling up here or down there, Chase?" Duncan pressed the munitions button then carefully selected his weaponry from the black tray hovering near his hand.

"Down there. Don't want my ship scratched." Chase set the ship down on silent thrusters. Then he unbuckled and stood, stretching once before adding an icevolgue to his holster. The pistol's ice shots would do well in close range, though he hoped to avoid that altogether.

A moment later, Watts and Myers emerged, suited up and ready to go. Iari stood beside Duncan, bearing only his trademark phaser. With a nod from Chase, they all descended down the ramp.

As Duncan looked over at Iari, an odd shimmer of blue hazed over the man's skin before it fused into his flesh. Sparks of white flashed in little dots and swarmed over Iari before they blended with the tone of his skin. *"Damn, how in the hell did he get an Electrical Graviton Aquainfuriator?"*

Once on the ground, Duncan moved to one of the twenty-foot posts embedded in the ground. There was a line of them stretching as far as the eye could see, spaced every hundred yards. Attaching a green band around its girth, the flux of AG seeding spilled into the air around them. It would attract CI to their exact spot.

"He's a king." Chase took the other side, stringing along the bands.

Iari hung back with Watts and Myers, looking far more ready than the two behind him. Myers and Watts were by-the-book and any little deviation irked them greatly. Chase couldn't stand the half-brothers, but damn, he loved screwing with their notions of protocol.

The barren landscape of the planet gave them few places to hide. One of the small AG rigs of metal and wood stood near the post, but it wouldn't provide any cover at all. As Chase finished the set up, Duncan scanned the sand and rocks. Only an outcrop of boulders would provide a decent spot to avoid getting shot at. Glancing over at Watts and Myers, he nearly chuckled at their twin looks of disgust. Motioning toward the stone, Duncan directed everybody to get behind it. Pulling out his comp-u-lator, he prepared the Mobius Ultrasonic Wave then glanced over at Chase.

Once everyone was safely hidden, Chase nodded. *"Bring 'em to us, babe."*

With a press of a button, a sonic wave eradicated their tracks, leaving the sand as pristine as it had before they'd stepped on it. The ripple flowed underground, appearing on the surface as it disrupted the sand. Duncan nodded to Chase and directed his hand-held at the rigged post. Blue clouds of gas filled the air.

"That's an unauthorized use of seeding, Captain Sykes." Myers looked over at Chase, frowning.

Chase shot him a scowl. *"Wise up, rookie. Just watch."*

"You think we should have sent CI a gilded invitation instead?" Duncan mocked him then fell silent as a dark sphere registered on his screen. *"Heads up. They're coming down. Cloak activated now."*

Chapter Three

A black, class B cruiser descended from the blood-red sky above them. Undetectable to its scanners, they waited for the ship to land. With a loud thrum, the cruiser's engines deactivated as it landed on the sand.

"Watts, Myers: get around to the rear, block any escape. Iari, Duncan, and I will take the front and sides. Now!"

As the men moved into position, the hatch of the ship opened. Three men slowly descended down the steps. The man in the lead carried himself with a noticeably noble bearing. They weren't that far from him and Duncan could see the downward slant of the outer corner of the eyes, the exact color of ripe plums. Long, straight, jet black hair fanned down over the white robe, reminding Duncan oddly of the petals of a flower.

"This is the bad guy? Damn, that sucks." Bemused, Duncan continued eyeing the number one enemy of Interferion.

"No shit." Behind the ship, Chase could see Watts and Myers, both of them looking less than thrilled. No doubt he and Duncan would hear a good bit about protocol once this one was done. With a curt nod from Chase, the plan was set in motion.

"His skills in sexual matters are unsurpassed." Iari's whispered thought reached all of them, making Duncan stare even more at the unquestionably beautiful figure known as CI as the etheral man glided across the sand.

As Duncan moved from the outcropping of stone, he had to drop the cloak to fire. Not quite willing to mar the perfection he was seeing, he chose one of the others as his target. A roar shook the land around them as the minion went down. Okay, Duncan had no idea the guard, concealed in a cloak, was a Zeroilidona.

"Well, fuck." Chase hadn't quite expected this. Quickly regaining some semblance of rational thought, he fired at the second guard, cringing when the ground shook beneath their feet. Two Zeroilidona. And a target neither of them had the gumption to shoot.

"Halt!"

Chase smacked his forehead and groaned when Watts walked around the ship, gun pointed at their target. "Fucking hell."

The only way to defeat a Zeroilidona was to do something to it that had never been done before. Gods knows what the hell that could be. Tentacles spread rapidly over the ground, coming toward Duncan as the other creature turned to stare at Watts, its huge mouth hanging agape. Well, that was one. Now for the other.

"Use the Divine Plywood Cry on it!" Duncan yelled at Chase as he raced toward the AG rig.

CI stood amidst the chaos with a confused air before another cloaked figure scurried from the ship and hastily dragged him back into it. Iari tried to intercept them, but he ended up trapped in a Lithoholder Trapperanoid. The blasts of his phaser cut away at the strands, but he couldn't free himself in time to stop CI's escape.

"It figures you'd yell for that!" Chase darted between tentacles, avoiding the slithering arms, and lunged for one of the loose wooden beams. With a hard tug, he pulled it out of the ground and spun around. He had only a second to land his blow, splitting the Zeroilidona's skull. The creature shrieked and hissed, its writhing mass dissolving into the ground.

Before any of them could react, the cruiser took off in a roar, ascending straight into the sky. Staring at the dissolving mass, Duncan started laughing before he moved over to Iari to help him. The other Zeroilidona stood motionless in front of Watts, frozen in pure shock.

Chase used every curse in the book—and several that would've made Arch blush—as he stalked up to the Zeroilidona. "Kill it or piss on it, but do something," he grumbled as he glared first the frozen creature and then Watts. He turned on his heel and headed back to the ship, brooding.

When Watts appeared too stunned by the creature's lack of action to do anything, Myers came up behind him and set fire to it with his phaser before he grabbed Watts' arm and dragged him back to the ship.

Following behind them, Duncan shot a look at Iari. "You knew, didn't you?"

"That none of you would be able to kill him? Yes, I knew."

"You could have warned me."

"And if I had?" Iari turned to face Duncan at the top of the ramp. "What then? Your captain is already angry. Is it because he was not expecting what you all witnessed? Is it because one of the most beautiful creatures in existence is also one of the most reviled by your government? Would it have made any difference if you knew?"

His riddles done, Iari turned and walked away, leaving Duncan standing at the ramp. From deep within the hull, the sounds of cursing and banging and general frustration rose. With a heavy sigh, Duncan traipsed into the ship.

"The Divine Plywood Cry? What the hell is that? Slapping somebody upside the head with a two by four is not regulation." Watts got in Duncan's face as he entered the deck.

"It worked, didn't it? Now shut the hell up and sit down, Watts."

Troubled by what he sensed under Iari's words, Duncan stared at the king as Iari settled in the chair near his.

A moment later, Chase walked onto the deck and dropped into his seat. He was covered in black grease. Tossing a blackened towel onto the console, he punched in the coordinates for...

"Hey. Where the hell are we dropping your rookie asses off?" He half-turned in his chair and eyed Watts and Myers.

"Commander Ryles posted us at Dagast in the Romeo quadrant, Captain Sykes," Myers answered him.

Duncan headed for his chair and strapped in. Iari gave him an enigmatic smile as he rested his hand on the metal arm of his seat. The slow stroke of his fingers drew Duncan's gaze.

"Dagast it is." Chase had the ship in the air in record time, his brain buzzing with too many thoughts and his body burning with too many needs. He could almost feel the way Duncan stared at Iari, the way Iari stared at them both. He imagined how it would feel to touch them both, to have them both touch him. God, he was so screwed. Or at least, that was the plan.

Finally, Duncan dragged his gaze away from Iari. With a couple of quick punches, he set the navigation system. "Coordinates in, Chase. Micro ten at Hydra set." Thankfully it wouldn't be too damn long before they got rid of Watts and Myers. With a smile, he looked over at Chase. "Next stop, Ionesphere?"

With a slow nod, Iari gave his agreement to the plan.

"Oh. Most definitely," Chase said with a wink.

"You need to file a report with Commander Talin, Captain Sykes," Watts piped in. "Regulation 127 of the Galactic Interferion code requires you to submit a full account of our encounter with CI."

Smirking, Duncan turned his head to eye the idiot. "And you want to tell them how fucking surprised you were when a Zeroilidona froze with your stupid ass command that you couldn't shoot it?"

That silenced Watts quite nicely.

* * *

Having finally dumped Watts and Myers off, Duncan relaxed in his seat, watching the Ionesphere come up on the vid screen. The entire planet was a hotel. Each section had its own bar and rooms that catered to the whims and fantasies of their clientele. The magnificent structure of the Ionesphere rose high into the air, carved from the planet itself. It had taken Con crews more than seventy earth-based years, and they still weren't done.

The Usicit Corporation had plowed through almost all of their entire capital on this one project. Naysayers had predicted the collapse of Usicit because such an undertaking had never been done. Duncan's grandfather had invested in Usicit, and twenty years later he became the richest man in Eala, thus securing for his family the right to rulership. It was a position that thankfully interested Duncan's youngest brother, leaving Duncan free to indulge in his own desires instead of having to run the family business.

As Chase and Iari made a quick trip to Ionioeth port for the specially recommended oils, Duncan viewed the choices popping up on his screen.

Half an hour later, Iari and Chase returned. Chase spun the navigator seat around and promptly straddled Duncan's lap, pushing his tongue into his lover's mouth without so much as a hello. Iari chuckled softly in the background, one hand landing on Duncan's shoulder, kneading the muscles gently.

Even used to his lover's antics, Duncan was surprised by the sudden hungry force of the mouth claiming his. Looking up questioningly at Iari, Duncan opened to Chase's assault, feeling the heavy grind of Chase's hips against his lap.

"Vanilla Ecstasy," Iari said, grinning down at Duncan. "We found some chocolate-covered ones as well." The very popular candy was a highly effective aphrodisiac and hadn't even been on the market very long.

Chase pulled back from the kiss, somewhat breathless and a lot horny. "Room. Need a room. Got the good shit, baby."

"Oh, Lord," Duncan muttered once his lips were free. Reaching around Chase, he set the nav system for the GS section of Ionesphere.

As Iari went to his chair, the ship began its descent. It was a damn good thing Duncan could do Chase's job as well. Especially since his lover probably couldn't think too clearly at the moment.

"Mm," Chase hummed, lips brushing over Duncan's ear. He tipped Duncan's head back and started kissing his throat. "Want you, baby. Deep inside."

A deep groan was Duncan's answer. He wasn't sure if they'd make it to the room he requested. His hands slid up into Chase's hair, roughly tugging his head back. A sharp bite of his teeth left marks on his lover's lower lip before his tongue pushed between them.

"Captain, we are approaching Section GS of Ionesphere," Mal's digital voice chimed in.

Chase pressed closer, sucking on Duncan's tongue, hard and steady. Panting, he finally pulled away. "Set 'er down, Mal," he said, licking his lips as he stared at Duncan like a starving man at a feast.

Chapter Four

"Just imagine," Iari purred softly as he stroked a finger over Chase's lips. Chase opened for him, eyes fastened onto Duncan's as Chase sucked Iari's finger into his mouth.

"Fuck, I am," Duncan muttered before he leaned just enough to flick his tongue against Iari's hand.

"We're docked at GS, guys." Mal's voice piped merrily over the com.

Chase released Iari's finger and slid off of Duncan's lap, pulling the navigator to his feet. "Come on. Now. Need you."

Hand tight around Duncan's and Iari trailing behind them, Chase led the way.

When the ship door opened, they walked the short white tiled corridor into the Ionesphere. White slender columns rising above the floor to the invisible ceiling surrounded the huge room. Above their heads, the darkness of space, littered with its millions of flickers of light, spanned the entire room. Heading toward the main desk, Duncan decided to bypass the bar.

"Duncan Sampson." After giving his name to the woman, Duncan took the holiscard she handed him.

"Third level, Mr. Sampson."

"Thanks." He led the others to the elevator platform. With a small whirr of sound, a black glass shield surrounded them and lifted them up to the third level.

Chase nuzzled Duncan and pressed close, stroking and petting Duncan's stomach. "God, you smell good."

"A kiss?" Iari asked him, turning Chase slowly.

Chase grinned and pushed against Iari, covering the ruler's mouth with his. Their moans filled the elevator as Chase rocked into Iari's body.

It seemed Iari wanted a taste of the captain. Duncan leaned against the smooth wall as his hand drew Chase's ass back against him. His teeth fastened to the side of Chase's throat, biting sharply at his skin.

Shivering and moaning, Chase moved between them, pushing back against Duncan as he opened to Iari's kiss. When the elevator stopped, Chase groaned in frustration as he pulled away. The doors opened and he took Duncan's hand, tugging him out of the elevator.

After checking the card for the number, Duncan headed for their room. Thankfully it wasn't too far from the elevator. Opening the door, he pulled Chase in with him into the Greek Isle fantasy. A lush garden of vividly colored flowers and white marble statuary surrounded them. Brick-lined paths led in different directions toward the Greek gods and goddesses flanking the garden. In the distance, a lake shimmered under the moonlight. Beyond that, a mountain spanned the horizon.

"The Greek States are always a good choice," Iari murmured as he closed the door behind them and it faded into the rest of the scenery, leaving only a single light to show where it was.

Tugging on Chase's hand, Duncan drew him toward a black, gossamer-draped tent. Inside, the floor was littered with plush pillows and several small tables laid out with a choice selection of fruits and wine. As he walked toward the tent, Iari pulled his tunic over his head, leaving him completely bare except for his boots. He stepped into the tent and stopped, arms crossed over a muscular chest.

"Oh. Oh, damn, Duncan... look..." Chase stilled in his work of stripping Duncan, mesmerized by the sight of Iari naked.

The sight of the muscular planes of Iari's chest had Duncan enthralled as he looked over the king's body. As much as he itched for his own taste of the intriguing jungle lord, Duncan doubted if Iari would go along with what he had in mind. After sliding Chase's jacket off of him, he unfastened the hook of the captain's pants, letting them drop to the floor.

Licking his lips, Chase tore his gaze from Iari to look into Duncan's eyes. "What do you want, baby?"

Iari moved closer to them and reached out to slide his fingertips down Chase's chest. Then he stepped up to Duncan and tilted the navigator's head back, covering Duncan's mouth with his own.

Unable to answer Chase, Duncan opened to Iari, and his tongue skimmed lightly between the king's lips. After a moment, he pulled away and stepped back to sit in one of the luxuriously cushioned chairs. "I'm going to watch you two."

Reaching for one of the glazed jugs, Duncan poured himself a cup of wine. As he took a drink of the sweet liquor, he watched them over the rim. Chase smiled slowly and Iari turned until Duncan had a good side shot. Then he pushed Chase to his knees.

"So hot," Chase murmured, hands and mouth sliding down Iari's chiseled body. When he reached the king's cock, Chase took it in one hand, lifted it, and rolled his tongue around the head. Iari groaned softly and slid his fingers through Chase's hair.

Watching the two naked and very beautiful men in front of him, Duncan slid slightly down, relaxing. "I fucking agree."

Lightly touching Chase's face, Duncan's finger drifted across his cheek to trace the lips wrapped around Iari's cock. When his finger inched over the king's hard flesh, Duncan smiled at the slight jerk of Iari's body.

Chase nuzzled Duncan's hand even as he swallowed Iari's cock. Iari's fingers tightened in Chase's hair and he started sliding in and out, fucking Chase's mouth with long, slow strokes. Without missing a beat, Chase glanced over at Duncan, his eyes showing everything he didn't have the words for.

The fragrance of the garden outside wafted on a gentle, warm breeze though the open flap of the tent. Pure erotic fantasy scented the air and excited the senses as Duncan lazily unfastened his pants. The smile on his lips softened as he met Chase's eyes. He knew how badly Chase had wanted to do the jungle king. Duncan was more than content to watch the sensual slide of his lover's mouth engulfing Iari, and Iari's expression of intent arousal.

Duncan's cock, already hard, sprang free of the confining material of his pants, and with a slow, sure rhythm, Duncan stroked himself.

Chase's gaze dropped to watch the slide of Duncan's hand. He moaned around the flesh in his mouth, vibrating the shaft. Then he turned his attention back to Iari. Gripping the king's hips, Chase encouraged the movements, speeding them up as Iari's thrusts grew stronger.

"Chase... yes... soon..."

A split second after he spoke, Iari's hips bucked sharply, driving his cock deep into Chase's mouth. Deep shudders followed as he came, shooting in the hot, willing mouth, drinking him dry.

Duncan stared at them and a low moan broke free from his lips, excited and aroused.

Chase licked Iari clean before letting the king slip from his lips. "Please," he pleaded breathlessly, hand dropping to his own cock. He looked over at Duncan, biting at his bottom lip as he watched Duncan jerk off.

"I think," Iari said, bending to kiss Chase softly, "that I would like to see you ride him, Chase. I want to watch you come with him deep inside you."

Knowing Chase was needing, Duncan shrugged out of his jacket and wriggled out of his pants. Without a word, he held his hands out to his lover. Later he wanted to see Iari fuck Chase, but now he wanted to satisfy the urgent plea in his lover's eyes.

Chase slid onto Duncan's lap and just as he leaned in for a kiss, two slick fingers slid deep inside him. He moaned into Duncan's mouth, rocking his hips and fucking himself on Iari's fingers.

Duncan's hand caressed over Chase's back then cupped the smooth curves of his ass, rubbing over it. He got one hell of a kick out of the anxious shift of Chase's body. When Iari pulled his hand away, Duncan's positioned his cock with one hand, and with the other, gripped Chase's hip. As he pulled his lover down, he thrust up to impale Chase in one hard, smooth move.

"Duncan!" Chase's head fell back and he ground down with his hips, shuddering as Duncan filled him.

"Yes," Iari whispered near Chase's left ear. "More, Chase?"

Chase nodded, gasping as one of Iari's fingers slid in alongside Duncan's cock. "Oh, fuck…"

Duncan's hand began to work over Chase's cock in a slow rhythm as he fucked him. The feel of Iari's finger along his cock sent a shudder through Duncan, taking away part of his control. Tipping his head back, he opened his eyes to stare into the mahogany ones of the king. Reaching up, he tugged Iari's head toward him.

As he bent for a kiss, Iari slid a second finger inside Chase. Then he captured Duncan's mouth with his, tongue fucking Duncan's lips.

"Oh, fuck," Chase gasped, body beginning to shake as he rode Duncan hard and deep. "Duncan… babe… Fuck!" Jerking and crying out, Chase came, ass squeezing Duncan's cock and Iari's fingers as he erupted over his lover's hand.

The movement of his lover's body riding him shot Duncan's control all to hell. As Chase came, Duncan did, too. Pumping hard into Chase's body, his cry was taken by Iari as the king hungrily consumed him.

When Iari straightened, Duncan raised his hand and licked the cream from his fingers.

"Damn." Chase panted and collapsed onto Duncan's chest. "Oh, man… that was awesome."

Iari chuckled and kissed Chase's hair. "I would agree."

"I don't think we're done with you yet, lover." Grinning wickedly, Duncan smirked at Chase before he looked up to wink at Iari.

"Umm, too true," Iari casually replied as his finger lightly slid up over the curve of Chase's ass.

Reaching over, Duncan kneaded his hand against Iari's ass as he pulled the king's hips slightly forward. A quick lick of his tongue wet the head of Iari's cock. Looking back up, he laughed. "It's going to be a long damn night."

Episode Two: And The Plot Thickens

Chapter Five

"Release the enormous berserk lemmings!" As he screamed, Rudolpho stayed well back from the portal as the gigantic furry hamster-looking creatures ran into the room. Apparently their arch nemesis remembered their last encounter, and the giant vampire assassin sheep.

Trapped in the warehouse's vat of quicksand, Chase couldn't move a muscle lest the sand swallow him further. When the humongous creatures reached the edge of the vat, the stampeding herd behind them pushed them head first into the sand.

"SHIT!" Rudolpho shrieked. "STOP! HALT! Dammit, Nerk!"

Chase was almost overcome with fits of laughter to catch the rope Duncan dropped down from the rafters. Finally pulling himself together, Chase grabbed the rope and let Duncan pull him out of the quicksand. The mass of fur surged into the sand, and the rodents scrambled over one another to get back out.

"Nerk! Where are you, you flat-headed imbecile?" Rudolpho shouted.

"The quicksand was your idea, sir," the small Riseon muttered at his boss as he leapt out of the way of the sand spilling from the vat. The sheer bulk of the lemmings had begun to displace the sand, causing it to pour out onto the warehouse floor.

On the platform overlooking the warehouse, Duncan yelled down at the poor, beleaguered Riseon. "Hey, Nerk, I'll double your salary!"

Looking upward, Nerk blinked at him. "What salary?"

"Hey!" Rudolpho attempted to reach Nerk, but the lemmings and sand surrounded him, keeping him in place. Nerk just smirked at him.

Once at the top, Chase scrambled onto the rafter beside Duncan. Looking down, he said, "Should we at least rescue poor Nerk?"

As the Riseon jumped up on a Nuc-Tam container to avoid the rising sand, Duncan glanced between Chase and Nerk, giving it a moment's thought. "Oh, what the hell."

After tying the end of the rope to the metal railing, Duncan tugged on the dangling length and tossed it toward Nerk. When the Riseon grabbed hold of it and began scrambling up, Duncan gave him a thumbs up.

"Give me that rope, you moron!" Rudolpho's shout went unheeded as Nerk climbed the rope, and Chase and Duncan dashed for the exit to get to their ship.

The angry yelling followed them out of the warehouse. Both of them were laughing as they raced into their ship. Soon as he dropped into his seat, Chase nearly doubled over. "Did you see the look on Rudolpho's face? I thought the man was going to bust a vein or two! Poor Nerk..."

Collapsing in his chair, Duncan erupted into gales of laughter. Gasping, he said, "He doesn't even pay poor Nerk. Did you get the Soul Bomber?"

Chase grinned and pulled the small, but highly lethal gun prototype out of his holster. "Little baby packs a lot of firepower."

The blue-black gleam of alu-steel glittered in the cabin's lights. "Damn. Fucking nice piece. Do we keep it or sell it? It's worth about five thousand creds."

"Think we can get away with selling it? Arch doesn't know about this one..." Chase's grin was positively wicked.

Arch's voice on the com broke in on their conversation. "You'll have it on my desk after you've safely delivered Ambassor Vilichr Kralycy to Tataimiuste in Quadrant Juliet."

"Damn, Arch, did you sneeze?" Grabbing the gun from Chase, Duncan tossed it on the ammuni tray. Puckering his lips, he blew Arch a kiss. "We still owe you for the intro to the jungle lord."

"You can thank me for that by behaving yourselves with the Ambassador," Arch said dryly.

"But... we always behave ourselves, Arch-baby!" Chase followed up by making several cooing noises at the com.

Leaning forward, Duncan smeared his lips on the com screen over Arch's face. "There ya go, sugar. It'll have to do 'til we stop by the home office."

"Seriously, you two. Ambassador Vilichr needs to arrive safely. If he doesn't, the Kralycy Army will retaliate. Be on the look out for CI."

Looking away from the vid screen, Duncan started to whistle innocently. When the last mission report had been filed with Central, none of the five involved had admitted they couldn't kill the unbelievably gorgeous creature known as Chaotic Insecure.

"Yes, Boss." Chase closed off the transmission and glanced over at Duncan. "He still doesn't know."

"He might if you don't shut up." Lifting his hand, Duncan made a zipper motion over his lips. The idiocy of Watts' actions hadn't appeared in the report, either. But then again, Duncan and Chase had agreed to keep their mouths shut about pretty much all of it.

"I'll give you something else to do with those lips, asshole." Chase smirked, leaning back in his chair and giving his crotch an exaggerated squeeze.

Sliding from his chair, Duncan muttered, "Best thing I've heard all damn day."

As Duncan knelt, he pushed between Chase's legs. Laying his hand on the bulge in Chase's pants, he kneaded the cock beneath. "Then we'll stop at Jezebel's for a drink before we get the ambassador. Mal, set a course for Jezebel's."

"Sure thing, Duncan." The cheerful voice answered him.

Chase stared down into Duncan's eyes, humming and nodding slightly. The man could con him into anything as long as he was doing that. Chase's hips lifted from the seat and his hands fell to Duncan's head, fingers sliding through his navigator's hair. "Sure, baby... just suck me and ride me."

With a quick twist of his wrist, Duncan had Chase's hard cock in hand and lowered his head. A lick of his tongue ran over the head before his mouth closed around it. His lips slid over Chase's cock with a tight suction that molded to the flesh.

"Oh, fuck," Chase groaned, his hands tightening in Duncan's hair. He let his head fall back and his eyes close, hips rocking slightly in the chair as he pushed up into Duncan's mouth. "Fuck, yes, babe. Gods, your mouth..."

Duncan devoured Chase with expert skill. His head bobbed up and down, teasing the fuck out of Chase with his teeth and tongue. As his mouth tightened around the head, he suckled at it before letting go. "I think you're ready now."

Standing, Duncan smirked and hastily stripped out of his uniform while Chase grabbed the lube.

Chase slicked himself, half-stroking, half-mesmerized by the sight of Duncan naked. Despite the time they'd been together, he never got tired of seeing that gorgeous, muscled body stripped bare.

"Come on, baby... slide that sweet ass down..."

Straddling Chase, Duncan eased the thick flesh into his ass. A quick push filled him with the penetrating friction. Not slow and easy this time, Duncan rode him hard, fucking wanting to get off.

While one of Chase's hands wrapped tight around Duncan's cock, the other tangled in the navigator's hair, tugging him down for a kiss. Hips bucking up in a furious rhythm, Chase shoved his tongue into Duncan's mouth, working his fist up and down the man's prick.

Duncan sharply bit at Chase's lips as his hands unzipped the captain's shirt. Running his fingers over Chase's chest, Duncan gave a painful twist to both of Chase's nipples. The escalation of pure need between them came to an explosive head. Coming in Chase's hand, Duncan's ass tightened on his cock with the hard grind of his hips.

Growling into Duncan's mouth, Chase jerked, cock throbbing deep inside Duncan's body as he came. He slumped into the chair, breathless and shaking through the last tremors. "Damn, babe..."

"Just keeps getting better, doesn't it?" Grinning at his lover, Duncan was quite happy to remain in Chase's lap for the time being. Their sex might be rough, but they adored each other.

Chase chuckled. "Always." He started to pull Duncan down for another kiss when Mal chimed in, letting them know they'd arrived at their destination. "Fuck."

"Just a quick one at Jezebel's." Duncan wasn't about to let Chase get away without giving him a kiss. Leaning down, he took what he wanted and didn't release Chase until he felt like it.

Quickly sliding off his lap, Duncan cleaned off before he put his uniform back on.

Laughing and shaking his head, Chase turned back around to the console. "I knew there was a reason why I loved you."

"The great sex, right?" Winking, Duncan leaned down and bussed a big, wet one on Chase.

Chase's answer was muffled by the oral assault. He simply returned the kiss, grinning as Duncan pulled away. It was the first time 'love' had ever been said; it was just something they both knew to be true without having to say it.

"Yeah, smart ass. The sex," he laughed.

With a smile, Duncan just had to say, "So when are you going to make an honest man of me, Chase? Or am I suppose to make an honest man out of you?"

All kidding aside, Duncan didn't look the least bit teasing.

Chase sat back in the chair after tapping in their course to take them down to the landing pad. "Name the time and place." From the way he smiled, it was clear he wasn't joking either.

Turning away, he opened the small com tray. After taking out a small black box, Duncan faced Chase and casually tossed it to him. "After we deliver Ambassador Vilichr."

Chase eyed Duncan and then the box. When he opened it, his mouth simply dropped open. "Duncan..."

Shrugging, Duncan tried to act like it was no big deal. "Love never dies. Just like the ring says, Chase."

Chase smiled and took the platinum ring out of the box. Turning it, he read the inscription: *Love never dies.* He stood and walked over to Duncan, sitting sideways in his lap. "Love you, babe."

Wrapping his arms tightly around Chase, Duncan looked up at him. "Love you, too, and for more than just the sex."

"Oh, yeah. The sex is just a fucking awesome fringe benefit." Chase winked and leaned down for a kiss.

"Docked, Captain." Mal's voice interrupted them.

After Chase got off his lap, Duncan readied his weaponry. Jezebel's could sometimes be a downright dangerous place. "Let's get that drink you promised me then we'll go take care of the Ambassador."

"That I promised?" Chase's laughter followed Duncan off the ship as Chase strapped his thigh holster into place. "Damn... this place got bigger, I think."

"Of course, you're paying, you know." Duncan nodded sagely as he strode down the ramp to the platform then headed into the bar. A rough looking lot of customers hung around the bar, and a few were dancing in a desultory manner on the dance floor.

"Hey, Jez." Duncan greeted the owner as he settled on one of the stools. "Give us the usual."

"Where you boys been? Haven't seen you in too damn long." Jez mixed their Octo Syrups as she talked to them. As a Rolaini, Jez could change gender whenever it felt like it. While they watched, Jez's body began to fill out and take on a more distinct muscle tone. Casually pulling off her shirt, the mounds of her breasts began to recede into the flat line of a masculine form.

Not a one blinked an eye.

"Oh, here and there," Chase said as he sat down beside Duncan.

Jez glanced up at him and grinned, bright pink lips rather shocking compared to his... her... purple skin. "Arch keepin' ya busy, I take it."

"Arch always keeps us too busy. Haven't been getting out much have you, Jez? You're looking a bit pale there." Duncan winked as he reached for the bright orange drink.

Pouting at him, Jez blew Duncan a kiss as he set Chase's drink in front of him.

A guy sitting near them looked at them and asked, "What exactly is it that you two do?"

"Whatever you want done," Chase said as he took a sip of his drink.

"Just not now, we're kind of in a hurry." Duncan smirked as he quickly downed his drink in one swallow. If you didn't drink it that way, the damn thing was way too painful on the throat.

Chase just shook his head and swallowed back his drink. "You're a wuss," he snorted at Duncan. "Come on. Let's get this over with. I have more important things to do." He gave Duncan a quick wink and stood.

The quick rush of the drink had Duncan's mind racing before his body could catch up. He fucking loved that sensation. Getting up, he grabbed Chase's hand and headed back to the ship. "I'm not really looking forward to this one. Playing babysitter to an ambassador is going to be fucking boring."

"No shit," Chase said as they hurried back to the ship. "So where are we picking up... whatever the hell his name is?"

"Ambassor Vilichr Kralycy. And he's going to Tataimiuste in Quadrant Juliet." Duncan sounded like he had a mouthful of marbles, when what he really would have preferred was Chase's cock.

Chapter Six

The Interferion terminal was jam-packed with bodies. Unfortunately, they were all alive. Chase and Duncan were jostled by other Galactic employees as they made their way to Commander Dopemei's office. Entering the room, Duncan held the door for Chase before shutting it behind them, muffling out the noisy chaos outside.

The Commander looked up from his desk, appearing ready to ream whoever had barged into his office. Taking one look at them, he just shut his mouth.

Ignoring him for the moment, Duncan made himself comfortable in one of the chairs and took a look at the man he assumed to be their guest for the duration. The ambassador had narrow, peach-color eyes that gleamed strangely as they fastened on Duncan. Vilichr's jade hair was bound in a series of braids tied at the ends by silver streams of light.

Lowering his gaze to the ambassador's delectable lips, Duncan smiled a bit. He found it all too easy to compare him to a dangerous bird of prey. The air of soulfulness contrasted oddly with the delicate serpentine movements of a slender body. Duncan's gaze traveled down over the tight sheath of the Ambassador's uniform. Little was left to the imagination since the material clung to every inch of the man.

Chase leaned down and whispered in Duncan's ear, "Remind me to thank Arch again." Then he straightened back up, one hand on Duncan's shoulder. "Good afternoon, Commander, Ambassador Kralycy."

Duncan barely stifled his snicker. They certainly seemed to be in luck lately with the choice assignments Arch gave them. As he stared at Vilichr, the man returned the favor, eyeing both of them. Duncan reached up to cover the captain's hand with his as he finally looked over at the Commander.

"When do we have to have the Ambassador to Tataimiuste?" Duncan couldn't resist a wink in Vilichr's direction before he turned back to Dopemei adding, "Sir."

"By tomorrow," Dopemei said dryly. "And do take care that he arrives there safely."

"There will be no worries there, sir." Chase pulled his hand out from under Duncan's and slowly grazed the back of his lover's neck with his fingertips.

"We'll get him there in one piece. Promise," Duncan answered quickly enough.

Addressing the two men, Vilichr filled them in on their mission. "I will be joining with the Risice delegation and giving them several seeding crystals. However, two have already gone missing."

"We are looking into that, Ambassador, and I deeply apologize for the mistake," the Commander said.

Bowing his head slightly, Vilichr accepted the apology gracefully. "As long as they are replaced. The Risice Ambassador is expecting to receive ten crystals."

Preferring to keep his eyes on Vilichr, Duncan watched the man as he talked with the Commander. No wonder the terminal was in chaos. If there were two missing crystals, heads would roll over it.

Patting Duncan's shoulder, Chase said, "Well, guess we better get going."

"Um, yeah." Duncan stood up.

"You'll have ten class Z star ships accompanying you. They'll be ahead of you, leading the ship position. I'm leaving you in charge, Chase. Don't let me down." With a minimum of words, the Commander got his point across.

Vilichr picked up the small black box of seeding crystals from the Commander's desk. When Vilichr followed Chase out the door, Duncan waited for a moment before falling in behind him.

"Is there anything you need before we board, Ambassador?" Chase glanced back at Vilichr.

"Everything I need should be on your ship by now."

Now that was a fine ass encased in shimmering tight green material. Duncan had an excellent view as they maneuvered back through the terminal to their ship. As if aware of the gaze, Vilichr looked back at Duncan and smiled.

It took Duncan a second to tear his gaze away from the enticing ripple of muscle beneath fabric. "It will be in a moment or two."

Chase choked back a chuckle as he stopped at the ship's ramp. "Your chariot awaits, sir," he said with a wave of his hand. As Vilichr started up the ramp, Chase hung back, angling his head just enough to get a good eyeful. "Damn," he muttered.

Duncan chuckled softly. "Isn't it, though? Who gets to show him to his cabin?"

"I will rest for a short time in your cabin, Captain Sykes. Please have my meal brought to me precisely at seven. You will both attend to me afterwards."

Looking back at Duncan, Chase lifted an eyebrow. "Guess that means me." He followed Vilichr up the ramp. "Yes, sir. Right this way."

"Mmm, demanding and forthright, too." Duncan chuckled as he headed toward the main deck.

"I know this isn't quite the accommodations you're used to," Chase said as he pressed his hand to the console screen. The door before them slid open and he motioned Vilichr into the room. "But I do hope you will make yourself comfortable."

"It will do nicely, Sykes." The strangely colored eyes remained fastened on the captain without even looking around the room.

Chase swallowed, unable to look away. Despite the man's beauty, something was just... odd about Vilichr. "If you need anything... at all, please don't hesitate to ask."

The tips of the ambassador's fingers delicately rested to Chase's cheek. "You and your navigator will provide that after I rest." A faint narrowing within the pupils of his eyes gave them a hypnotic quality.

His voice lowering to a whisper, Chase nodded absently. "Yes, sir."

"Chase, they're done loading the cargo," Duncan's voice came over the com.

Chase shook his head quickly, snapping himself out of the bizarre space his mind had been in. Pressing a button on the wall, he said, "On my way." Looking back to Vilichr, he smiled. "Your meal will be ready shortly, sir."

"Thank you, Sykes." Stepping toward the bed, Vilichr started removing his uniform as Chase left the cabin.

Chase hurried back up to the bridge and closed the door behind him. "Okay. Is it just me, or is there something really weird about the ambassador?"

Busy setting the navigation coordinates, it took Duncan a moment to glance over at Chase. "Weird? Other than the green hair and orange eyes?"

"Weird... as in something not quite right." Chase shook his head and walked over to the captain's chair, dropping down into it with a sigh. "Maybe it's just me."

"It's been a long day. Kick back and relax. I've got something to make you feel better." Grinning at his lover, Duncan started unzipping his uniform.

* * *

Duncan tried to get a bit of a rest, but when it proved to be fruitless, he left the cabin and headed to the engineering bay. Since he couldn't sleep, the least he could do was get a bit of work finished. In the bay, he unfastened the covering of the Tactical Probe-Deflector. It had been out of commission since they left the home base, and both he and Duncan had put off putzing with it.

Reaching for a pair of gloves, Duncan put them on before he slid his hands down between the ghastly green glowing orb and the slick sides of its container. Gently, he tried to spin the orb, but it refused to budge. After several minutes, it still wouldn't move. Duncan eyed the wrench nearby, debating about hitting it.

"Star class B cruiser docking now."

Duncan didn't pay any attention to Mal on the system com. Hearing the whir of the bay door, Duncan had to look around a massive metal pillar to catch a look at Vilichr. The man might be a pain in the ass, but there was definitely another type of pain Duncan would love to encourage.

As the outer bay door opened, a cloaked figure stepped through. One momentary glimpse of the pale face nearly stopped Duncan's heart. When the ambassador reached for the other man and hugged him, Duncan's mouth dropped open.

What the hell was going on? Though Vilichr obstructed Duncan's full view, Duncan couldn't have mistaken the face. It was CI.

From the folds of his robe, Vilichr pulled out something. Duncan could see the blue glow of the seeding crystals pulsing even though he couldn't actually see the crystals. Apparently the crystals that had gone missing weren't actually missing.

Quickly passing them to CI, Vilichr bowed his head before he stepped back and hastily left the bay. None of what Duncan saw made sense. Why was the ambassador, the staunchest supporter of Interferion, helping CI?

The concealed figure began to turn back to the bay doors, then he stilled. Lifting his hand, CI's fingers beckoned in the direction of Duncan.

God of Asussius, he was in trouble. Duncan didn't know how CI knew he was there, and wasn't really sure why his feet started moving. As Duncan came out from behind the pillar, CI lifted his hands to lower the hood of his cloak.

Impossibly exquisite. Duncan's breath caught in his throat with the thought. The most unusual plum-colored eyes held his, and Duncan was enthralled.

"You won't betray me, will you, Duncan?"

As Duncan stilled in front of the most hated man in Interferion history, the soft, dulcet whisper made him shiver, and the certainty in CI's tone surprised him. CI's voice caressed over his senses, drawing its own reaction from him.

Feeling the light touch of CI's finger underneath his chin, Duncan's eyes widened, not knowing what to expect. In the next moment, the brush of CI's lips stunned him, and he opened without rational thought to the tongue seeking to learn him.

Duncan couldn't help but press closer to the body near his as his arms slid around CI's neck. Lust, but something beyond that as well, guided him. He understood this man would be important to him, but how? Why? Duncan couldn't hold to his thoughts as he tasted the rich, creamy flavor of CI's mouth. The kiss was tinged with Diusid, one of the rarest candies in the known universe.

CI ended the kiss, not Duncan. As he drew back, Duncan saw CI's skin was no longer pale but had become a delicate blue. *From the crystals?* His brain struggled to hold any coherent thought as he gazed into CI's eyes.

With the press of his finger against Duncan's lips, CI smiled softly at him. "No, you won't betray me."

Turning, CI walked through the bay doors and back into his ship. The quiet metallic sound of the doors shut behind him and still Duncan didn't move. He made no attempt to raise the alarm or to stop CI.

"Disengage the Psychic Gate Chain in five... four..."

Duncan heard the numbers, but still didn't react as he should have. The memory of the kiss burned into him and he couldn't reach for the alarm button nearby.

"Two... one... disengage."

"What just happened?" Since there was nobody around to hear his question, Duncan didn't get an answer. Bemused, he finally went back to the Tactical Probe-Deflector, but he only replaced the container lid before he left the bay.

Chapter Seven

Instead of heading to the deck, Duncan walked down the back corridor to Chase's cabin. When the door opened for him, he saw the captain locked in an embrace with Vilichr. Damn, the man worked fast.

The door shut behind Duncan as he stepped into the room. Without waiting for an invitation, he quickly shed his uniform before he moved up behind Chase. The scene was too great of a temptation. One hand brushed the hair back from the side of Chase's throat before Duncan's teeth fastened in a light grip to his flesh.

Chase groaned, the sound muffled by the ambassador's mouth. Reaching behind him, Chase slipped a hand between his body and Duncan's, fingers curling around Duncan's cock to arouse him further.

Vilichr's hands were busy as well, stripping out of his robe, then divesting Chase of his clothing. Duncan did his part to help as well. Before Chase realized it, he was caught between two very gorgeous, muscular men. The gods must have loved him at that moment.

A moment later, Duncan nudged into Chase's hand as he returned to nuzzling the captain's neck. The cool feel of Vilichr's hands ran over them both, sending shivers down Duncan's spine. The ambassador moved toward the bed, pulling Chase toward him with an insistent pressure. With a soft hissing sound, Vilichr stopped at the edge of the bed.

"I will have you."

Chase nodded, caught in the ambassador's mesmerizing gaze.

"We both will." A definite command lay beneath Vilichr's silky soft voice.

Eyes wide, Chase opened his mouth to speak, but when Vilichr stretched out on the bed, tugging Chase to straddle him, Chase found he honestly had no words. After grabbing for the lube on the dresser, Duncan tossed it to Vilichr with a wicked grin. The ambassador caught the tube and opened it to smear the liquid on his rigid cock. Vilichr's skin was a lighter shade than his hair, and the sight of the tall rod standing at attention was incredible. With a gentle push, Duncan shoved against Chase to get him into the position both he and the ambassador wanted the captain in.

Chase was already beyond speech. He knew exactly what was going to happen. They'd talked about it before, but this was the first time for it. With one hand on his hip, Vilichr lifted Chase just enough to probe his hole with the tip of his long, slender cock. One determined push of his hips and Vilichr slid deep inside Chase. Chase's head fell back as the ambassador's cock settled inside him.

Moving up behind Chase, Duncan really didn't give him time to think at all. His hand cupped beneath Chase's ass, caressing over it as he slicked some of the lube on his own prick. Duncan slowly worked his fingers alongside Vilichr's cock, then he pulled them out and began to inch inside Chase. "Double the pleasure, baby."

A strained but pleasured sound emerged from Chase's throat. Panting, fingers digging into Vilichr's chest, Chase was nearly shaking as Duncan's cock pushed deep. The fit was tight, filling, and Chase's body and mind screamed at the stretch, but gods, it felt fucking good.

"Duncan..." His voice came out hoarse, desperate, as Duncan was seated inside him, squeezed tight against Vilichr's cock.

On one knee, Duncan used his foot for balance. It required some coordination to pull this one off. The tight fit drew groans from both him and the ambassador. Duncan's hands rested heavily on Chase's shoulders as he whispered, "Feels so fucking good."

Vilichr groaned in agreement as he slowly moved inside Chase. The feeling pulsed through Duncan and when the ambassador stilled, he rocked tightly to Chase's ass before he pulled slowly out then back in.

Chase could only ride the sensations, fingers flexing against Vilichr's chest, digging into his teal skin. Duncan and Vilichr were alternating strokes, never leaving Chase empty as they took turns filling him over and over.

As they slid against each other inside Chase, tremors rolled through Duncan with the feel of the incredible fiction, near to driving him insane. Without a word spoken, they increased the speed, each cock pushing into Chase's ass at regular intervals.

Duncan lost it first. His come filled Chase's ass as he pressed tightly to his captain. His shout of pleasure echoed in the small cabin and Vilichr followed shortly after, the chill of his seed pouring inside Chase.

Nothing existed but the two pricks throbbing deep inside him and Chase roared, his entire body jerking as he came. As his cock spurted without a single touch, his ass clamped tight around the men filling him. Panting and exhausted, he collapsed onto Vilichr's chest, completely heedless of the mess.

All of them were breathless as they became motionless, needing time to unwind from the intensity. Duncan pressed a soft kiss to Chase's shoulder before he slowly eased out of him.

With an unexpected gentleness, Vilichr nuzzled in against Chase's throat, and a whisper soothed over the captain. Chase murmured softly and didn't move. Vilichr's hands stroked slowly down his spine to ease the captain's strained and sore body.

"I think we broke him," Vilichr chuckled.

"I guess that means we'll have to do our damnedest to fix him." Settling at the edge of the bed, Duncan's hand ran alongside Vilichr's as he winked at the ambassador.

"We have all night to do that, Sampson. Neither one of you are leaving this cabin until we've reached Tataimiuste."

Chase hummed his agreement, nodding his head slightly as it rested on the ambassador's shoulder. "Won't hear us complaining," he mumbled. Slowly—very slowly—he eased up and off, dropping down onto the small bed beside Vilichr. "Damn."

Making a mental note to send a requisition form to Arch for a bigger bed, Duncan leaned over and silenced the ambassador with a kiss of his own. His hand slid over Chase's hip and to Vilichr's thigh, the tips of his fingers lingering in a caress against the cool teal skin. They'd keep each other busy for what was left of the night, and Duncan knew damn well none of them would get a minute's sleep.

Chapter Eight

Chase set the ship down nice and easy. The port was surprisingly quiet, not as busy as normal. Shrugging, he stood and went into the galley. "We're here. Do you have everything you need, Ambassador?"

As Vilichr slipped on his golden mantle, it unfortunately hid the trim figure beneath. Their playful companion of the night before was gone, in his place stood the cool, commanding figure of the ambassador. "I am ready."

Duncan eyed him for a moment with a grin before Vilichr walked toward the docking bay. Nudging Chase, he whispered, "I think I prefer him naked."

"I heard that." The ambassador looked over his shoulder at them and winked.

Chase chuckled and nodded. "I couldn't agree more." They followed the ambassador off the ship and toward the main hangar. "Where is everybody? I've never seen this place so deserted," Chase muttered.

A sudden burst of noise filled the hangar as several people came out of their hiding places, yelling, "Congratulations!"

Their boss, Arch, stepped forward, bringing an Asochisi priest with him. A grin, stretching from ear to ear, plastered Arch's lips. "We're all here to make sure neither of you skips out."

"Holy shit!" Duncan stared in complete shock as everybody he knew came out of the woodwork and crowded around them.

Chase's mouth simply dropped open. He stared over at Duncan. "How did you manage this?"

"Me? I thought it was you." Dumbfounded, the only thing Duncan could do was blink as his hand was shaken repeatedly.

"No..." Chase smiled and shook more hands. "If it wasn't me and it wasn't you, then who..."

Right about that moment, they both turned to look at Vilichr. The ambassador's unabashed grin widened, giving him the look of a cat with canary feathers. Folding his hands behind his back, he said, "Congratulations, gentlemen."

"You? How in the hell..." Duncan trailed off, shaking his head in total amazement.

"I overheard both of you. It was a relatively easy matter to arrange everything, and your friends wanted to be in on it."

"All right, you two, take your places." Arch grabbed them both by the arms and dragged them toward the priest. "All of us have been waiting a long time for you two to settle down."

Chase laughed and went quite willingly. When they stopped before the priest, he looked over at Duncan. "Ready, baby? Think you can live the rest of your life with me?"

Duncan took one look at Chase and didn't even need to answer that question. Taking Chase's hand, he pressed a soft kiss to the back of it before they turned to face the priest. Behind them, everybody gathered in a half circle as the room became silent.

"We are gathered today to witness the union of Captain Chase Sykes and Navigator Duncan Sampson. These two men have shown undying loyalty to one another, and now they are here today to seal the bond between them." The priest looked from one to the other. "Are there rings?"

Duncan had one, but it was on the ship. "It's on the cruiser. I didn't expect..."

Hurriedly he dashed away and ran into the ship. It took him a moment to remember where the hell he'd put it. Opening the com tray, he snatched the box out and pulled the ring from it. Not sure what to do with the box, he tossed it to the ground before he sprinted back to the ceremony.

Chase chuckled softly, smiling over at him when Duncan came flying out of the ship. Then he looked at Arch. Their boss stepped up to him and placed something in Chase's hand. When Arch stepped back, Chase turned and held up the platinum wedding band, giving Duncan a shrug.

"I always knew it would happen at some point."

Trying to catch his breath, Duncan eyed the ring and muttered, "Smart ass. You could have told me you already had a ring for me."

"Duncan, place the ring on Chase's finger and repeat after me: This ring is my pledge of our eternal bond."

Taking the captain's hand, Duncan slid the ring onto his finger, and he couldn't resist drawing it upward to kiss the ring. "This ring is my pledge of our eternal bond."

With a beaming smile, the priest looked at Chase and repeated his instructions.

Chase smiled and, without looking away from Duncan's eyes, he slipped the ring on Duncan's ring finger. "This ring is my pledge of our eternal bond." Instead of letting go of Duncan's hand, however, he threaded their fingers together, holding on tight. And if there was a tear or two... well... no one but Duncan saw them.

"I officially announce the bond between Chase Sykes and Duncan Sampson. Congratulations, gentlemen. You are married. The blessing of Asochisi graces your union."

With the words, the short but sweet ceremony binding them was finished. Cheers erupted behind them as Duncan pulled Chase to him. With a grin, he murmured, "It's your job to take out the trash and mow the lawn now." Before Chase could say anything, Duncan's lips molded over his in a brief, hard kiss.

Chase wasn't about to let Duncan go yet. With Duncan's hand still in his, Chase used his other hand to grip the back of his navigator's head, deepening the kiss. Only when he was satisfied did he let Duncan go. "Love you, baby."

"Love you, too." With Chase's hand in his, Duncan turned to face the happy greetings from their friends.

"It's about time," Arch said, slapping Chase on the back.

"Yeah, guess we're both gettin' too old." Chase grinned over at Duncan before his lover was pulled away to chat with another group of friends.

Grabbing for Chase's hand, Duncan dragged him along. After the champagne was popped, they both were handed glasses of the sparkling liquid.

"To the happy couple." Arch led the toast, lifting his glass toward Duncan and Chase.

A chorus of "here, here" answered him as Duncan deliberately entwined his arm with Chase's and tried to drink from his glass. After spilling the bubbly, he had to lick at his lips to clean it off.

Chase leaned in and helped, laughing as their tongues dueled for the remnants of the champagne. He finished off his own without mishap and released Duncan's arm to set the glass down. When he looked up, Arch was standing in front of them.

"So, any ideas of where you two will go for a honeymoon?"

"Well, that depends on how much time you're willing to give us off, old man." Duncan smirked at him as he set the glass down on a nearby tray. With his hand free, he slipped his arm around the captain, hugging to him. "A month off would be real nice."

Arch rolled his eyes and the dry tone of his voice could have parched the Musonop Ocean. "You've got a week. Then I expect your butts on Ycega for your next assignment."

"Hm, I think we can get into sufficient trouble in a week." Chase winked at Duncan, slipping his hand down to cup his lover's ass and giving it a squeeze. "Don't you think so, baby?"

"Oh, I think we'll find plenty to amuse ourselves." Smirking, Duncan wiggled slightly against the hand. "At least Arch won't be able to listen in."

"Half the time listening in is the only way I find out what you two are really up to." Arch was on a sarcastic roll.

"Half the time you don't want to know what we're up to, Arch." Duncan winked at him.

"That's true, too."

"There are just some things a man does not tell his boss, no matter how good a friend said boss is," Chase said, then laughed. "Trust me."

Arch eyed them both dubiously, but he didn't say anything more about that. "Now, about this honeymoon..." He fished around in his pockets until he came up with two envelopes.

Then he handed one to Duncan and the other to Chase. "Enjoy yourselves, boys. You have a week."

Taking the envelope, Duncan opened his. When he saw the credit amount, he looked quickly at Arch. "Damn, Arch, how'd you swing that?"

Arch smiled and shrugged. "What can I say? You two are my best."

Chase remained silent, too stunned at the tripled amount of a normal paycheck.

"Now you two get out of here and enjoy the week off." Arch rested his hands on their shoulders and turned them both around before shoving them toward their ship.

To a hail of "good luck", Chase and Duncan headed for their ship as they were pelted by kernels of rice.

They turned and waved to everybody before the ramp lifted. When the hatch was secure, Chase turned to Duncan. "Where are we going anyway?"

"I've got a planet all to myself if you're in the mood for nobody around us in the star system." Grinning, Duncan headed for his seat and waited to see if Chase gave his okay to the idea.

Chase smiled and walked over to the com. Switching it to autopilot, he sat down in his seat and turned it to look at Duncan. "As long as I can have you all to myself for a week, I'll go anywhere, baby."

"We're married, you know that? We'll just have to be a boring old married couple now. It's legal." Duncan teased him as he set the coordinates then settled back in his seat, leering at Chase.

Chase slid out of his seat and knelt in front of Duncan, running his hands over his husband's thighs. "We are," he said with a nod. "You remember when we first met?"

"I think I was rather drunk at the time. But I remember you picked me up at the Black Hole on Jonu. Don't think I've forgotten that." Duncan's expression softened as he reached out to him, smoothing his hand against Chase's hair then downward over the line of his throat.

Chase closed his eyes and lost himself in his lover's touch. "Took you home with the intention of a one-night stand." He opened his eyes and looked into Duncan's. "Glad you stayed for coffee."

"It's not often a man finds somebody like you, Chase. I just had to keep ya." Leaning forward, his hand slipped beneath Chase's chin, tilting it up slightly. "I'll never find another like you."

"Better not," Chase mumbled, licking at Duncan's lips. "I'd have to kill him. I'm selfish, you know."

Laughing, Duncan made a face at him. "You know better than that, love. You're the only one in the universe who'd put up with my faults."

Chapter Nine

Glancing over at the navigation screen, Duncan checked their position. "It shouldn't be too much longer before we arrive on Phesis."

"Good." Chase rose slightly, bringing their faces closer together. "Want you, baby. Want you naked, in a bed, where I can worship and taste and touch every inch of your body, inside and out."

With the words, a surge of lust ran through Duncan, hardening his cock. A faintly rough edge colored his words. "We have a whole week to enjoy each other. And there'll be nobody but you and me."

"Phesis ahead, guys," Mal's merry voice interrupted.

"Thank you, Mal." Chase gave Duncan a light, teasing kiss and moved back to his own seat. He took Mal off auto and started the descent through the Phesis atmosphere. He was almost squirming in his seat, visibly anxious.

Equally as impatient, Duncan waited until the ship landed. The house he owned on the planet had been built to overlook the shore of the Bestan Sea. They definitely wouldn't be disturbed here.

The minute the ship touched down, Duncan came out of his chair and took Chase's hand, pulling him out of his.

"You'll love this place. I just know it." When the ramp descended, Duncan headed out with Chase in tow. The first thing that hit them was the fresh, clean scent of sea air. "It's been too damn long since I've been here."

Chase breathed deep and smiled. "Oh, man... this is awesome, baby."

The house itself resembled something out of a deserted isle dream. The low, sprawling building gleamed in the midday sun and looked entirely deserted. Tugging on Chase's hand, Duncan pulled him down the path then paused to press his hand against the door pad. After the door unlocked, it swung open and they both went inside.

The darkness of the room lightened as one of the draperies across the far wall opened for them. Sunshine spilled into the room, bathing it in a golden glow. "There's a pool out back if you prefer that over the sea," Duncan said. "And the bedroom is the last door in the back."

"C'mere." Chase pulled Duncan up against him. "Shower, baby... then bed."

As Duncan's arms wrapped around Chase's waist, he walked backwards toward the hall. "Welcome to our home, love. One of us should have carried the other over the threshold."

"Oops," Chase chuckled, steering Duncan toward the bathroom. Then he stooped and picked Duncan up, stepping through the doorway and into the oversized bathroom. "Close enough."

Laughing, Duncan gave him a quick kiss. "You can put me down now."

Chase set him down and bent to turn on the water in the shower. As the spray warmed up, he started stripping, watching as Duncan did the same. Gods, he could never tire of looking at the man.

Duncan put on a bit of a show for Chase as he slowly undressed. After tossing his uniform into the hamper, he ran his hand along Chase's backside before he stepped into the shower. "No Arch, no Interferion, no Rudolpho, no assignments. This is definitely my idea of perfection."

Chase didn't answer until he got in and pulled the curtain closed. Pressing Duncan against the tile wall, he whispered, "Now it's perfect."

A small rumbling noise answered Chase as Duncan leaned against the wall. Resting his hands on Chase's hip, he kept him flush against his body. The spray of hot water poured over them, but Duncan seemed oblivious to it as he stared into Chase's eyes.

"God, you're fucking gorgeous," Chase whispered, touching Duncan's lips with his fingertip.

The tip of Duncan's tongue tasted his husband's finger. A play of emotions reflected in his eyes before he spoke softly. "I don't think I tell you how much I love you often enough. But most times, I don't really have the words for what I feel."

"I know, love. I've always known." Chase pulled his hand away and leaned in, kissing Duncan softly. "With everything I am, I've always known," he murmured.

As his arms slid around Chase's neck, Duncan answered the kiss. His tongue slipped slowly inside Chase's mouth, stroking in a tender caress, the motion an unhurried exploration of what Chase offered him.

Moaning softly, Chase rested against Duncan, sliding both hands through his lover's hair. Tipping Duncan's head slightly, Chase deepened the kiss, taking his time as he suckled on Duncan's tongue.

Duncan's fingers played beneath Chase's hair at the nape of his neck as they savored the flavor of each other. Only the need for air broke them apart. Duncan rested his forehead against Chase's and drew a deep breath. "You're my entire world, Chase, and the only one I truly want in it."

Chase smiled, drawing back to kiss Duncan's forehead. "Always." He lowered his head and nuzzled his lover's neck, licking away the drops of water, shivering with the taste. He moved over Duncan's throat, licking and kissing, knowing the hidden spots that started a blazing inferno... and the ones that sparked a slow-burning flame.

A slow shiver betrayed Duncan's reaction to the feel of Chase's lips and tongue. Tilting his head to encourage his lover, his hands ran slowly over Chase's shoulders and down against his back. The light drag of Duncan's nails pressed into him, kneading every inch he could reach. Reaching for the soap, he ran it over Chase, lathering his skin as he began to wash each intimate part.

Chase hummed softly, the sound vibrating over the smooth skin of Duncan's neck. "Feels good, baby." He caressed Duncan's shoulders, down his biceps, fingers tracing every muscle. He shivered when Duncan's hand brushed over his stomach, bringing the rest of his body to full attention.

Duncan's hand began to slowly soap over Chase's cock before he shifted forward to circle his fingers around both of them. Slowly running his hand up and down both of their cocks, he drew back his head to watch Chase.

A shiver moved up Chase's spine and he rocked against Duncan. "Baby... Duncan..."

After letting the water rinse them off, Duncan turned off the shower and grabbed a towel. His other hand continued pumping over their cocks as he leaned forward, nipping at Chase's lip.

Chase finally forced himself to pull away. "Gotta stop," he panted, "otherwise I won't last long enough to play."

Chuckling, Duncan handed a towel to Chase and got another one for himself. As he dried off, his gaze lingered on his lover, and Duncan couldn't resist an occasional touch.

Once they were both relatively dry, Chase pointed to the bed. "I want that sweet body spread out like a buffet."

A smirk twitched at Duncan's lips before he headed toward the bed. "You realize that means I'm gonna lay here and let you do all the work."

"That's the idea," Chase said, gaze fastened to Duncan's ass. He waited until Duncan was stretched out on his back, then he crawled onto the bed, settling between Duncan's legs. Leaning down, Chase started at Duncan's left thigh and moved up slowly, soft kisses and licks teasing his husband's skin.

Duncan parted his legs, giving Chase ample room, and simply watched him. The butterfly touches started a slow burn and his cock twitched in reaction. Raising his arms behind his head, he propped himself for a better view. "Right now, all I can think about is how much I love you and how fucking gorgeous you look."

Chase hummed distractedly, nibbling his way up Duncan's inner thigh. "Love you, baby," he murmured. When he reached the juncture where Duncan's thigh met his groin, Chase bit down, at the same moment, sliding his hands up to grip Duncan's hips.

Duncan's hips lifted slightly from the bed as he groaned softly. Needing to touch, his hand moved to Chase's, covering it. He tried to subdue the more urgent need pulsing through his body, but wasn't sure how successful he would be.

Bypassing Duncan's cock and balls completely, Chase drew a line over the crease of Duncan's hip with his tongue. "Turn over," he whispered. "Wanna taste." He smiled slowly. "Wanna play."

"I know I'm in trouble when you say that." Obligingly, Duncan's leg swung over Chase and he shifted onto his stomach before stretching out on the bed again. The wide spread of his legs gave Chase ample access to him, and Duncan shivered in anticipation of what was to come.

"Oh, hell yes..." Chase knelt between Duncan's legs, running his hands up Duncan's thighs, over his buttocks. He kneaded them, spreading them apart, hands positioned so that his thumbs pressed just on the outside of Duncan's hole. "Want to see that sweet ass spread open, slick, aching for me." He leaned down and flicked his tongue over the pucker. "Want to fill you up, stretch you."

The words alone suddenly increased the tension in Duncan's body. Duncan could only answer him with a low moan as his ass arched for Chase's attention. Burying his face against a pillow, he reached back, grabbing a hold of his ass cheeks to open himself. As he rocked slightly, his cock rubbed against the blanket beneath him, adding more friction.

"Yeah," Chase groaned, sliding down. "Hold that sweet ass of yours open for me. That's it, baby..." He gripped the Duncan's ass, spreading the cheeks further apart. Then he leaned in, pushing his tongue into Duncan's hole as deep as he could go.

A strangled groan fell from Duncan's lips as his body trembled. Rising on his knees slightly, he held his ass open and up for Chase, feeling the tongue plunge inside him. Throbbing sensations raced straight through him, leaving him in a deep aching need to feel a lot more.

Chase licked and sucked on the puckered skin, loving the heat and tightness. Pulling back slightly, he sucked a finger into his mouth and slid it into Duncan, hissing with the sensation. "Fuck, you're hot, baby. Want more?"

Duncan's "uh huh" was the only thing he could manage as he squirmed back against that finger. Resting back on the bed, he humped against the rougher friction of the blanket to arouse himself even further. Finally he gasped out, "More, babe, more."

"Lube," Chase said, working his finger in and out. "Wanna open you up, feel everything..."

Only moving just enough to open the drawer on the headboard, Duncan fumbled around and got the lube. Reaching back, he handed it to Chase. Already highly on edge, he waited impatiently for Chase to touch him again as he continued the excruciating rock of his hips on the bed.

Chase pulled his finger out and slicked three. Tossing the lube onto the bed, he worked all three into Duncan, leaning over his ass and kissing his spine. "So good, baby," he breathed across Duncan's skin as he pushed his fingers deeper, spreading them apart.

Duncan's breath caught in his throat as he felt the intimate stretch of his body. It triggered tremors all the way through him and drew ragged, deep noises from him. Knowing Chase was watching added another edge to his pleasure.

Adding a fourth finger, Chase twisted his hand, working Duncan open. "Want inside, Duncan," he whispered.

Knowing exactly what Chase wanted, Duncan nodded in agreement as his hips pushed back into the more filling sensation. With the near painful stretch as Chase pressed inward, Duncan focused on complete relaxation, stilling to allow Chase inside.

Tucking his thumb in, Chase pushed slowly and gently, twisting his hand slightly as the other rested on the small of Duncan's back, rubbing lightly. He drew in a breath as Duncan's body sucked him in, the ring of muscle squeezing his wrist as his hand was buried inside his husband's body.

"Oh, sweet fuck," he breathed.

"Chase." The name hissed between Duncan's teeth as he felt Chase's whole hand settle in him. A small inner twist of the hand sent lightening rippling along his nerve endings, and a harsh groan followed. Slowly he began bucking against Chase's fist, and the sensations burst over him. When he came, he nearly passed out from the intensity dragging him under. Pulse after pulse released in his body, and shortly after he shot on the bed, barely aware of the sticky mess beneath him.

Chuckling softly, Chase eased his hand out and reached for one of their towels from their bath. He wiped his hand off and cleaned Duncan before lying beside him. "Love you, baby." He stroked his fingers down Duncan's back.

Duncan remained limp on the bed, incapable of movement. His eyes still had a dazed quality as he opened them to look at Chase. Words weren't coming out of him yet so he made sounds instead. "Umm hmm."

Chase grinned. "Been wanting to do that for a long time. Thank you."

Finally, Duncan managed to get on his side, resting his hand on Chase's hip. "Welcome, but I think somebody else needs to be taken care of."

Shifting again, Duncan draped his leg over Chase's hip, pulling him close as he leaned in for a kiss.

Humming softly, Chase opened to him, drawing Duncan's tongue into his mouth, sucking on it gently. "Want you, Duncan. Love you so much. Need you."

Drawing out the kiss, the slide of Duncan's tongue pushed deeper into Chase's mouth. Rolling over, Duncan settled on him, never breaking the kiss. The slow path of one hand ran over Chase's chest as the other grabbed blindly for the lube still on the bed.

Chase spread his legs, letting Duncan settle between them. Hands cupping his lover's face, Chase poured everything into the kiss, hips rocking slightly to slide their cocks together.

The movement ignited Duncan's arousal as he pressed back against Chase. His fingers sharply twisted Chase's nipple, tugging on it as he lifted his head. "I'm gonna hear you beg first, love." Turning his head, he latched onto one nipple, suckling and biting as his fingers worked the other.

Chase's breath left him and he arched, pushing his chest toward Duncan. "Fuck!" His hands gripped Duncan's head, fingers tangling in his hair. "Baby... oh, fuck..." He moaned and rocked, gasping with every sharp bolt of sweet pain.

Uncapping the lube, Duncan squeezed the gel onto his fingers and didn't care when some got on the bed as well. Lowering his hand, he used one finger to tease lightly against

Chase's hole. His mouth and fingers continuously tugged at Chase's nipples, lavishing a great deal of attention on them.

"Baby... Duncan..." Another twist to his nipple and Chase saw stars, lightning shooting from his chest to his cock. "Sweet fuck, Duncan, don't stop." He rolled his hips, desperate.

A finger eased inside Chase, drawing out the moment before another entered him. Grazing over his prostate, the movement of Duncan's fingers stretched his ass. Releasing one nipple, Duncan used the lube again, slicking it over his cock, preparing himself as he nibbled at the other hardened nub.

Before Chase could react, Duncan pulled out his fingers and positioned his hips to slowly penetrate his ass. Lifting his head, Chase watched Duncan's face intently, drawing pleasure from the desire he saw in his husband's eyes.

Chase's gaze locked to Duncan's. There were no words left, nothing he could say. Duncan knew it all. Wetness began to pool in Chase's eyes as Duncan slid deeper into him. Chase fell in love all over again.

Duncan's emotions were an open book to his husband, nothing ever hidden. It surrounded them and voiced itself in the gentle lovemaking between them. The drift of Duncan's hand lingered over the bare skin beneath him as the slow rock of his body repeatedly took Chase.

Chase resisted the urge to close his eyes. Instead, he watched Duncan, drank in the pleasure as it moved through his lover's face, drowned in the love in Duncan's eyes. Reaching up, he touched Duncan's lips with a fingertip, tracing the curve slowly.

"I'm lost in you," he whispered as the tears slipped free.

Pressing a soft kiss to Chase's finger, Duncan spoke softly, "I'm never going to let you go, love." The inexorable build of need between them strengthened with the joining of their bodies, and the tender caress of Duncan's hands intimately roamed wherever his touch would reach.

Fingers sliding into Duncan's hair, Chase pulled him down for a slow, deep kiss. That was all it took. A whimper and shudder, and Chase came, crying out into the kiss as he shook beneath Duncan, heat spreading between them.

A moment later, Duncan fell with him, both of them shuddering in each other's arms, locked together, sharing the world of passion between them. They were all each other truly needed. No matter who else came in and out of their lives, it would always be them together.

Episode Three: What The Hell Is Going On?

Chapter Ten

"Release the invisible, crazed, throat-ripping squirrels!" Rudolpho's mad scream reverberated through the warehouse, and Nerk hurriedly obeyed the command. A horrific sound followed as the portal opened, but none could see the enemy coming.

Duncan scrambled from his position to get to the Unstable Lithoholder Astrosmoker. Hoping to confuse the oncoming horde in a noxious cloud of the gas, Duncan quickly punched buttons to get it started.

Suddenly Rudolpho shrieked, a high-pitched note that came near to shattering glass. Slapping wildly at his pant leg, Rudolpho danced around. Apparently he didn't see the enemy coming, either.

Turning to look at him, Duncan shouted, "Damn, Rudy, you sound like a girl!"

Rudolpho ignored him, still doing a jig on the warehouse floor. "Nerk! Damn it, Nerk!"

"Yes, Rudy... err... sir!"

Seconds later the massive bay doors of the warehouse exploded, raining rusting metal across the floor.

"Hey, it works!" Chase shouted from the other side, an enormous grin plastered on his face. He waved the H.r. Time Bacterial Ejaculator at Duncan, then his eyes widened as Rudolpho ran past him, legs high-stepping like a show horse on speed.

Rudolpho bent, picked up a nearby metal rod, and flung it at Duncan. Caught off guard, Duncan didn't seem to be in his usual stride and the rod connected with the back of his head. Without a murmur, Duncan collapsed to the floor in a heap.

Cackling gleefully, though in pain, Rudolpho threw himself to the ground, rolling in an attempt to squash the gnawing squirrels attached to him.

"Duncan!" Chase raced to Duncan's side and struggled to lift him while still holding the weapon. When he felt the weight ease somewhat, he looked up to see Nerk. "What the..."

"I'll help you carry him," Nerk said, gaze flicking over to where Rudolpho still struggled on the floor.

Blinking, Chase just nodded and together they steadied Duncan onto Chase's shoulder. "Thank you." After they carried Duncan to safety outside the warehouse and set him on the launch pad near the ship, Chase asked, "Why don't you ditch the idiot and join us?"

Nerk shrugged and smiled. "Rudolpho is an idiot... but he's my idiot." With that, he turned and walked back inside to help Rudolpho. Seemingly able to see the damn invisible squirrels, Nerk weaved and jumped around the room to get to his master.

"What the bloody hell was that about?" Chase dragged Duncan up the ramp and, as soon as they were in, he slammed his fist down on the button to close the door. "Mal, get us up!"

Out cold, Duncan apparently didn't feel a thing as the captain hurriedly drug him into the main cabin. When Chase finally got him propped up in his chair, a low groan came from Duncan and he opened his eyes.

"What the..." Stopping abruptly, Duncan's hand went to the back of his head. "Fuck, that hurts."

"Whoa, easy, babe." Chase knelt in front of him and pressed an ice pack to the back of Duncan's head. "He gotcha good."

"I've got a lump the size of Phicrthal. When did his aim get that fucking good?" Wincing at the cold, Duncan reached around Chase to get one of the All Purpose Nitraphenabumentol caplets from the med tray.

"He didn't," Chase said quietly. "You weren't paying attention. I think the bigger question is: what's eatin' you, babe?"

Downing the pill with a drink of water, Duncan focused on Chase, then lowered his eyes. "I was trying to get that damn Astrosmoker going. First time one of my plans didn't work."

Slipping a finger beneath Duncan's chin, Chase tilted his head back up. "Bullshit. Talk to me, Duncan. What's wrong?"

Reluctantly meeting the gaze pinned on him, Duncan sighed. "I wanted to tell you before, but the timing was wrong. Before we dropped the ambassador off on Tataimiuste, I saw him in the bay. I was working on that stupid Deflector."

"What about him?"

The words came out in a rush as Duncan hurriedly tried to get to the point. "You remember those seeding crystals that were supposed to be missing? I saw him give them to CI."

Chase's jaw dropped. "What?"

Wincing at Chase's expression, Duncan lowered his gaze again. "There's more. After the ambassador left, CI knew I was there. I don't know how he did. He kissed me, Chase. I..."

Falling silently, Duncan appeared to be at a loss for words and confused as hell to boot.

"Okay... lemme get this straight," Chase said, sitting back on his heels and running fingers through his already disheveled hair. "Two crystals, valued a good hundred thousand more credits than ten ships like this combined, are not missing, and have indeed been given to Interferion's worst enemy?" He blinked and shook his head. "I'm not sure which is more noteworthy: the crystals... or your lucky ass getting a kiss from CI."

Duncan gave a startled laugh at Chase's offhand comment. Leave it to his captain to see it that way. "I don't know, Chase. I should have raised the alarm, I knew it. But I just couldn't, and I really don't know why. He was on the ship. But he knew I wouldn't do anything to him."

Chase blew out a breath and looked up at him. "Did he say anything to the ambassador? Hell, did he say anything to you?"

A frown wrinkled Duncan's brow as he tried to remember everything. "They didn't say anything at all. They just hugged and the ambassador gave him the crystals. I'm not sure why Interferion's biggest supporter would do that. The only thing CI said to me was 'you won't betray me'. And he was really damn sure I wouldn't."

Silent for several seconds, Chase finally said, "Ya know, babe, I wouldn't either."

Nodding slowly, Duncan sighed then spoke quietly. "I get the feeling something isn't right. I don't know what it is, but something really doesn't feel right. It has to do with him, Chase. I just don't know what."

"Ever get the feeling you're on the wrong side?" Chase asked quietly.

"I don't know, Chase. I'm starting to wonder. Why does he have to have those crystals so badly? I don't think it's the value of them. It's hard to explain, but I think he gets energy from them."

"Normally, I'd tell you you're nuts and need me to just fuck some sense into your head," Chase said. "But honestly, I believe you."

Duncan's breath released in a relieved sigh. "It's been driving me crazy, love. I wanted to tell you. But we suddenly got married, and I really didn't want to say anything during our honeymoon."

Chase rubbed his hand over Duncan's thigh. "You think we should tell Arch?"

Laying his hand over Chase's, Duncan shook his head. "I don't think we should. We don't have any proof of anything. And you know Arch. What's the first thing he'd say?"

Chase rolled his eyes, cleared his throat, and did his trademark Arch voice: "You boys got any fucking proof?"

Laughing, Duncan added, "And if I say, well, it's a hunch, he'd throw us out of the office."

Chase snorted. "Wouldn't be the first time."

"You wanna risk it? We risk enough stealing little trinkets from old Rudolpho. And by any chance, did you get it in all the excitement?"

"Yeah, I got it." Chase stood and dropped a quick kiss to Duncan's lips before leaving the room. A few minutes later, he returned. He handed Duncan the weapon and knelt in front of him, resting his arms on Duncan's knees. "As for Arch..." He sighed. "I don't know."

No longer interested in it, Duncan tossed the weapon on the med tray.

Out of the blue, Arch's voice came from the com. "As for me, what? Whatever it is, I want it on my desk after you get back from Meonen. Mijon's command captured Beast, and you two are his escort to the Lymusiadus prison on Vius. Oh, and boys, welcome back from the honeymoon."

"Babysitters again, Arch?" Duncan's voice had a complaining edge to it.

"Yes," Arch said simply. "Arch out."

Chase reached over and made damn sure the com was off. "Welcome back to work, eh?" He grinned up at Duncan, hands inching up his navigator's thighs. "Wonder if Beast is as hot as his mug shot..."

"I've heard of him but never seen him." Duncan's attention was no longer fully on the conversation as he slid down a bit in his seat to edge Chase's hands up higher. "Wanna give aid to an injured man, love? I'm badly wounded and need some tender, loving care."

"Got an aching head, babe?" Chase moved his hands up, fingers tracing the crease of Duncan's hips through his pants.

Playing it up for all it was worth, Duncan murmured, "Mmm hmm." Tugging at the fastenings of his uniform, Duncan wiggled to get out of it. "It's hurting all over."

"Wanna play doctor?" Chase's grin was positively wicked. "Let me examine you, fix those aches?"

"I think I need some proper medical help, and you're the only one here to give it. Course, you do need to get naked to give me some, now don't you?" Duncan kept a completely straight face during the whole thing.

"On the contrary," Chase said, tugging Duncan's pants down and off, "I can't examine you properly if *you're* still dressed." Grabbing Duncan's hips, Chase pulled him down further into the chair and pushed his legs up until Duncan's knees were near his head. With a bit of awkward squirming and some hasty tugs, they got Duncan's uniform off.

"Fuck yeah, babe. You got the right idea." Helping him, Duncan's hands moved to his thighs, holding his legs up. "You're going to have to check me out real good. Just to make sure you don't miss anything."

"It's appears, Mr. Sampson, that I'm going to have to do an internal exam." Chase reached up and fumbled with a drawer under the console until he found the lube. Slicking two fingers, he rose up on his knees, licking the drops pearling at the tip of Duncan's cock as he pushed two fingers deep inside him.

Whatever Duncan might have replied was lost to the low groan emerging from his throat instead. A wiggle of his hips pressed onto Chase's hand, increasing the arousing sensation as his cock twitched against the touch of Chase's tongue. The line from his brain to his cock ran on one track, and Duncan needed to be fucked. Another groan fell from his lips with his words. "Oh fuck, babe, stop teasing."

"Anything, baby," Chase muttered. With his fingers still buried in Duncan and his other hand working his pants open, Chase angled his head down slightly and sucked the head of Duncan's cock into his mouth. Giving it a long, sucking kiss, he finally let it slip free and pulled his fingers out. A quick stroke to slick his cock and he rose up, thrusting into Duncan with a deep groan.

Already hard, Duncan grabbed his cock when Chase entered him. His fist pumped at a frantic pace and Duncan grunted, hips bearing down as best he could. A wild rock of motion worked his body into a frenzy of need. Duncan stared up at Chase, need rushing through him in a large explosion of sensation. Streams of come spurted over his hand and his ass clamped tightly around Chase.

"Oh, fuck yes," Chase groaned. He gripped Duncan's hips and started slamming into him, jerking Duncan onto his prick with every hard thrust. Seconds later, he growled out Duncan's name and shot deep inside him.

Duncan floated in the haze, his hips ground tightly to Chase. A moment later, they both started to come down. With a lazy smile Duncan murmured, "Love you more than anything, Chase."

"Mm, love you, too." Chase eased Duncan's legs down and leaned close for a slow, easy kiss.

Chapter Eleven

Duncan worked busily at the console, calculating the nearest course to Vius. Unfortunately, even the shortest route there was more than a day away. When he heard the rattling of metal, he looked over his shoulder to find out what was going on. Behind him, two Interferion guards flanked an incredibly gorgeous man who would have made a parched man drool. The man was shackled from neck to ankles. The first thing that hit Duncan was the wild mane of silver curls, and the rest of the Beast seemed just as untamed.

Intriguing aquamarine eyes held Duncan's gaze for a moment before Duncan took in the rest of Beast's body. Other than the chains, the man wore only a pair of form-molding gray pants. Duncan could see a lot scars on the smooth, muscular body and he felt sure there had to be quite a story there. He could only be thankful they hadn't dressed the man in Interferion's disgustingly drab prison wear yet.

Chase wandered in and squeezed past the guards and their prisoner. "I've set up a storage room in the hold for..." His words trailed off when he turned around, eyes going wide. "Damn."

One of the guards had a harried expression and addressed them both. "Where do you want this guy?"

Smirking, Duncan wanted to give the obvious answer, but he settled back in his chair, enjoying his own eyeful of the prisoner.

Chase walked over to Duncan and popped him on the head. "Duncan, why don't you show our 'guest' to his quarters?"

Startled out of his reverie, Duncan jumped up from his seat. "Yeah, sure. Just leave him with me, guys. I'll handle it."

With a motion of his hand, Duncan shooed the other two off then moved to escort the prisoner to his new quarters. Looking back at Chase, he winked mischievously before he left the main deck.

He didn't say anything to the prisoner, though he wondered what the hell the guy was guilty of. Only the worst on Interferion's roster would be that heavily chained. Duncan had to keep his steps slow so the prisoner could keep up with him. Instead of taking him to the hold, however, he changed direction toward his own cabin. He didn't use it anyway and at least it would be far more comfortable than the cramped hold.

Duncan kept his curiosity to himself as he glanced several times at the man. Each time the blue eyes meet his, a shiver rippled through Duncan. Damn, those eyes could either freeze a man's soul or warm the hell out of it.

Opening the cabin door, Duncan gestured for him to enter then shut the door behind him. Returning to the main deck, the navigator decided to do a little investigating of his own.

Chase looked up from the com after putting Mal on auto. Spinning the chair around, he said, "Okay. Is it just me, or is there something fishy going on with our new guy?"

"He seemed awfully quiet and docile to be chained like that, and his eyes were too clear, so he wasn't drugged up." Settling in his chair, Duncan started typing on the computer keyboard. "Personally, I'm very curious about our guest."

Leaning to peer over Duncan's shoulder, Chase murmured, "That makes two of us, 'cause the only time something that hot needs chaining is if it's in our bed."

"What a coincidence. That's the same thing I thought." Reading quickly over the text on his screen, Duncan frowned. "What the—?" Pointing to one of the paragraphs, he asked, "You reading this?"

Chase blinked, his mouth dropping open. "Well, now..." He leaned closer. "Question is: was it stealing?" He looked up at Duncan. "Or getting them for someone?"

"A vague reference to an association with CI and trying to steal crystals. Now why does that sound familiar? But why the hell is he so heavily chained and being sent to Vius? That doesn't make sense. A guy like that would get killed there."

"They're trying to keep him locked down, not for crimes, but from CI?" Chase offered. "Call it a gut feeling, love. Our prisoner has definite ties to CI."

"Your gut feeling matches mine, and I think a talk with him would come in handy. You coming?" Turning off the screen, Duncan looked over at Chase.

"Yeah. Yeah, I think I will." Chase followed Duncan down to the navigator's cabin, giving Duncan only a mild smirk. "First class accommodations, eh?"

"Hey, I didn't want to put the poor man in the hold. It's too damn cramped in there." Laying his hand on the ID screen, the door opened and he stepped inside.

Their prisoner was stretched out on Duncan's bed, staring up the ceiling. He didn't say anything, though he turned his head slightly, watching them as the door slid closed. Chase went over to the chair at Duncan's desk and sat down.

"I hope you find your surroundings comfortable," he said in his best diplomatic, non-threatening tone.

"Oh yeah, I'm comfortable as hell."

Grinning at Chase, Duncan made himself comfortable at the foot of the bed. "Got a couple of questions for you. Wanna tell us why you were trying to steal seeding crystals?"

The man eyed them both with a wary look. "I have my reasons."

"Look, we're not guards," Chase said. He leaned forward, resting his arms on his knees. "We're just escorts."

Duncan cut quickly to the chase. "You were stealing them for CI, weren't you? Just like Ambassador Kralycy. Only he didn't get caught, but you did."

The expression of pure shock on the prisoner's face rewarded Duncan's effort. Stammering, he could barely get out the words. "H-how did..."

"Duncan's a master at finding out things most people shouldn't know," Chase said quietly. "We know the ambassador, quite well. But stealing crystals isn't enough for them to shackle a man from head to foot. What is it about you that makes you such a dangerous figure to Interferion?"

Duncan gave him a long look over before he said quietly, "Yeah, I want to know why you're being sent to the worst prison in this damn universe. You don't look like a mass murderer to me. You look more like you'll be a dead man very shortly after we get to Vius."

Abruptly the prisoner sat up and dropped his feet to the floor. "The trial was a mockery. Interferion wanted me out of the way. End of story."

"Why?" Chase asked him, giving him a stern look. "What sort of relationship do you have with CI that makes you so fucking dangerous?"

Dropping his gaze, the man remained silent for a long moment. Folding his hands in his lap the rattle of his chains accompanied the movement. "I'm his brother. My name is Silas. They found out. I don't know how."

"Shit." Duncan's eyes widened. Lately everything just seemed to get deeper and deeper when it came to CI.

"That explains a lot." Chase glanced over at Duncan. "A hell of a lot."

"We kept it quiet," Silas continued. "But someone obviously found out and when they caught me stealing the crystals, well..." He held up his hands, the chains making his point clear.

"Yeah, it does." Standing, Duncan moved toward Silas and hooked one of the chains with his finger. He dug in his pocket with the other hand and pulled out the key, then proceeded to unlock the chains. Silas stared at him, speechless. Duncan just smiled a bit before he knelt to unfasten the ankle chains. When he finished, Duncan tossed the metal to the corner of the room.

"What are you doing?" Silas blinked, a nervous but curious gaze shifting from Duncan to Chase, then back to Duncan.

"Just believe us when we say that we know better," Chase said simply.

"Relax, Silas, we're not going to hurt you. We have our own interests." With a grin, Duncan cupped his hand against Silas' cheek and slowly leaned forward. "Right now, I just want a taste."

He fell silent when his lips brushed softly across Silas'. Knowing the poor man was probably confused all to hell, Duncan made the effort to relax him. A small gasp sounded from Silas and Duncan took advantage of it. The gentle push of his tongue slipped into Silas' mouth, teasing. For a moment, Silas just sat there, stunned. With a little more coaxing from Duncan, however, he began to return the kiss, tentatively searching out Duncan's tongue with his.

"Damn." Chase's whisper sounded almost loud in the small cabin.

Pleased with the small reaction, Duncan let Silas take his own taste before he slowly pulled back, smiling. "We really won't hurt you, Silas. I swear." He reached back for Chase's hand and held it. Standing, he motioned toward the door. "Now, why don't you join us for something to eat?"

Silas just nodded and stood. "I assume you both are..."

"Yes, we are," Chase answered him with a smile. "We just came off our honeymoon, actually."

"Married?" Silas asked, following both of them to the galley.

"Yes, we are, and I'm in the mood to whip up something fancy." While the other two settled at the table, Duncan opened the Expando-fridge. He pulled out several covered trays and set them on the table. The whole time he eyed Chase with a wide grin.

Chase leaned over to whisper in Silas' ear. "When he gets that look, it's probably best to worry," he chuckled softly.

Uncovering each tray, Duncan recited some of the rarest dishes in the universe in a dramatic voice. "Roast Althesian boar, Talfar soufflé, Vesci fruit from Lareuret Seven, and..."

Pausing for effect, he reached back into the fridge and pulled out a dark bottle. "Snalket wine."

Silas stared wide eyed at the feast laid out in front of them. "Is he rich or something?"

Chase snorted. "Sometimes I wonder myself, and I've known him for countless years now."

"Well, dig in, guys." After getting plates and utensils, Duncan sat down next to Chase. "Just a special feast for the love of my life." Pouring them all a glass of wine, Duncan lifted his in toast. "To new friends."

Shaking his head and grinning, Chase lifted his own glass. "To new friends."

Silas followed suit, although a bit tentative. "To new friends."

After sipping his wine, Chase hummed in appreciation. "Oh, babe. That's wonderful."

"Only the best for you." Leaning toward him, Duncan gave Chase a quick kiss. After setting his glass down, Duncan helped himself to a generous portion of everything.

Filling his plate as well, Silas looked between the two of them, obviously trying to figure them out.

Eyeing him back, Duncan grinned. "Yes, I know. We're unfathomable. Don't bother trying to understand. Just eat."

"Don't worry," Chase said as he filled his own plate and started eating. "Not even our own boss can figure us out half the time.

They fell into a companionable silence, Silas periodically glancing between them. During the course of the meal, Chase rested his hand on Duncan's thigh casually, just petting.

After he took the last bite, Duncan set down his fork and turned slightly to lean back against Chase. Reaching for the wine, he poured himself another glass. "You're part of our world until we figure out what we can do for you, Silas. So just relax and enjoy the ride."

Chapter Twelve

Settled back on the main deck, Duncan and Chase worked on the maintenance levels of the ship. Pausing in the middle of adjusting the Broadcast Messenger-Communicator, Duncan looked over at Chase. "Love, if I suggested something, would you hear me out before you said no to the idea?"

Chase just stopped what he was doing. "It scares me when you ask shit like that. What's your idea?"

"I'm thinking about calling in a few favors and getting Silas off the ship." Duncan kept his gaze on Chase the whole time he spoke.

One eyebrow arched and Chase's gaze narrowed. "You realize that we aren't known for losing anything."

"It might mean some discipline, but I'd rather take that than drop Silas off in a place where he'll get killed." Shrugging, Duncan turned his attention back to his job. "If you'd rather be out of it, I can drop you off at Stagherst before it happens."

"Excuse me?" Chase dropped the wrench and twisted around, pinning Duncan down to the floor. "You think, for one minute, that I'm going to go anywhere?"

"No, but I was making the offer." Looking up at Chase, Duncan spoke quietly. "I'd understand, you know."

"Have you lost your mind? Duncan, I love you. We're in this together, clear?"

A smile creased Duncan's lips. "Through thick and thin, love?"

Chase settled on Duncan and lowered his head, lips brushing Duncan's softly. "Through everything, baby."

With a gentle nip, Duncan tugged at Chase's bottom lip then released it. "But did you sign on for some of my more completely out of my mind ideas?"

"Mmm, long as you keep doing that," Chase rumbled, "you can have all the hair-brained ideas you want."

Inching his hand between them, Duncan's fingers played over the front of Chase's pants. The sound of a small cough distracted him and Chase looked up to see Silas standing in the doorway.

Chase groaned softly, head dropping to Duncan's shoulder. He rocked slightly, just barely pushing against Duncan's hand. "You wanna bring your idea up now?"

"Hey, Silas, wanna join us?" Duncan winked at him before he lifted his head slightly to lick Chase's lips. He slowly wiggled his hand over Chase's cock, not giving him a chance to get away.

Chase bit down on an exposed bit of flesh where Duncan's neck met his shoulder. "Want you," he whispered, soothing the bite with his tongue, "deep. Wanna ride you."

"Fuck, babe." Duncan completely lost track of what the hell was going on other than the sound of Chase's words and the soft plea. Getting rid of Chase's clothes became top priority and Duncan didn't give a fuck who was there. Impatient fingers pulled at Chase's uniform, getting it off in bits and pieces.

"Come on, baby," Chase panted, helping to get rid of his clothes. He leaned down and took a kiss, tongue pushing into Duncan's mouth as need began to override everything else.

"Sweet fuck." The whisper came from the doorway just as Chase's ass was bared. When Duncan glanced quickly over at Silas, he noticed the young man was a great deal closer to them, watching them with a sharp intensity. Both of them were already naked, and Duncan definitely wouldn't mind if Silas were the same.

"Lube, babe." Duncan whispered to Chase, continuing to watch Silas. His gaze slowly drifted down over the clothed form as a faint suggestive smile curled his lips.

Chase fumbled for the lube they kept stashed in the toolbox. Managing somehow to get it open and two fingers slick, he reached back and pushed both fingers deep inside himself, hips rocking against Duncan.

Silas groaned and the sound of a zipper followed. "Fuck, you two are…"

Fingers digging into Chase's hips, Duncan lifted him slightly and positioned his cock with the other hand. A smooth upward thrust of his hips drove him deep inside Chase and both hands clamped tightly onto the captain. "Ride me, love, and suck him off. I want to watch."

Silas' eyes widened before he hesitantly stepped forward, closer to Chase. Chase threw his head back, grinding down hard on Duncan. Reaching out, he wrapped his fingers around Silas' cock and pulled the man close, tongue sliding up the shaft before he sucked Silas down.

The sight above him and the sensations within his body drew a deep groan from Duncan. He couldn't look away from the view of Chase's mouth sliding back and forth over Silas' cock. One hand released Chase's hip to play with his cock, and a hard grinding thrust kept Duncan buried in the tight, willing body. "Fucking beautiful, babe, fucking beautiful."

A deep throated moan from Silas followed, seemingly in agreement, and his hand moved to Chase's head. Chase groaned, rocking and grinding against Duncan, fingers digging into Duncan's chest. He moved his mouth up and down Silas' cock, licking at the tip, then dropping back down. Silas grunted and both hands gripped Chase's head, his hips thrusting forward.

"Gonna come," Silas rumbled. Chase made a desperate noise and nodded, humming around the prick in his mouth as he rode Duncan hard. Seconds later, Silas roared, pushing deep into Chase's throat as he shot.

Duncan didn't miss a second of it. His fingers tightened around Chase's cock, jerking him off, and the movements of his hips became near brutal as he fucked Chase. It took little more and Duncan came with a shout of pleasure, filling Chase's ass.

Barely able to catch his breath, one of Silas' hands grabbed for a nearby shelf to support himself. He slipped out of Chase's mouth just as Chase shouted, cock pulsing in Duncan's fist. Breathless, Chase dropped onto Duncan's chest, shaking.

"That... was... a first," Silas said in-between breaths.

Sliding his arms around Chase, Duncan held him tightly, giving him a chance to come down. The tips of his fingers drifted gently over Chase's back in a soothing touch. Duncan being Duncan, he simply couldn't resist commenting, "Hopefully not the last, Silas."

Chase's chuckle matched Silas' and he mumbled, "No, shit," against Duncan's shoulder.

"I should hope not." Silas grinned down at Duncan as he tucked himself back into his pants.

"Think we ought to get dressed and talk to Silas?" Duncan asked Chase.

"Talk to me about what?" Silas asked.

Chase nodded and sat up, unable to bite back the soft groan when Duncan's cock shifted inside him. "Yeah. Yeah, I think we should."

Duncan slapped Chase's ass and whispered, "Later, babe. After we talk to Silas."

When Chase got off of him, Duncan grabbed his clothes and any nearby rag to wipe off. Then he stood and put his uniform back on. Silas sat in one of the chairs near the console and watched them expectantly.

Chase cleaned off and dressed, then sat down. "I'm gonna let Duncan take this one," he chuckled.

Joining them, Duncan settled comfortably in his own chair. "You're not going to Vius, Silas. That's already been decided. Be a damn shame to waste a body like yours in that place. Right, babe?" Duncan asked his husband, grinning like a banshee.

"Not going to...? What do you mean?" More than a touch confused, Silas' gaze moved between the two of them.

Chase snorted and sat back in his seat. "Leave it to my dearest love to get another insane idea, but yeah, he's serious, Silas. You'd be eaten alive out there and I promise you that it wouldn't be as nice a job as we could do."

Leaning forward, Duncan began typing on the console keyboard. He didn't say anything for a few moments, concentrating on the screen. After nodding to himself, he finally looked over at them both. "You're going to escape, Silas. It's already been arranged. A friend of mine, Av Jeril, will be docking with us in a couple of hours. He'll take you wherever you need to go. And if you need a place, I have one of those."

"I..." Silas blinked. "I want to go back home, back to Cyril."

"To who?" Chase asked.

When Silas hesitated in his answer, Duncan had an idea he already knew who Cyril was; he had a gut feeling. "You mean CI, don't you, Silas?"

Silas nodded slowly. "CI are his initials: Cyril Illurian."

"Damn." Chase looked over at Duncan. "Is it going to be possible?"

Staring contemplatively at Silas, Duncan considered the options before he slowly nodded. "Silas should be able to get a message to him once he leaves the ship. Av would have no problem going anywhere."

Admittedly, Duncan would pay through the nose for it, but he kept that fact to himself. Directing a look at Silas, he said quietly, "Just keep our names out of it, all right? You escaped and that's what you tell everybody. Even CI."

"I'll be indebted to you," Silas said. "Both of you."

"It's Duncan's ship," Chase said. "It's his ass that'll get fried if word gets out. You keep quiet, and we'll call it even."

"Yep, and you'll be there to lather on the burn cream, babe." Grinning, Duncan got up and motioned toward the door. "Now, how about a few hours of R and R before Av gets here?" Without saying another word, he left the main cabin, heading for Chase's quarters.

Chase just flashed Silas a grin and stood. Following Duncan out, Chase wolf-whistled at the bemused young man. "Can't wait to taste that sweet ass."

Silas just groaned, adjusted himself, and followed along for the ride.

Episode Four: Death By Zombies

Chapter Thirteen

"Release the genetically-engineered, single-minded cyborg sharks!" The echo of Rudolpho's mad shriek bounced off the walls of the newly redecorated warehouse.

Nerk, his ever obedient sidekick, dashed to the Displacing Porter console and opened the portal for his master. Several large splashes followed and dark menacing shapes slunk through the water.

"What the—" Duncan walked into the ground level section and unexpectedly fell into the swimming pool. Floundering, he sunk beneath the water, and a few seconds later his head broke the surface. "Who put a damn pool here?"

Rushing to the edge of the pool to watch Duncan get eaten, the barefooted Rudolpho ended up skidding across the smooth tile and into the pool.

Chase snorted, but the laughter was short-lived when he saw the fins. "Oh, fuck. Babe, out. Now!" He extended a hand down to Duncan, helping him to the side as quickly as possible while Rudolpho screamed in the background. Only the gods knew what the moron was accusing Nerk of this time because Rudy was damn near incoherent.

Before Duncan could grasp Chase's hand, an Armed A.I. Assault Grappler grabbed Chase from behind, pinning him against the cold metal of its chassis.

"Nerk, shut it off! Shut the damn thing off! Drain the pool! Do fucking something!" Rudolpho bellowed as one of the sharks circled him threateningly.

Duncan did his best to scramble out of the pool, but the slickness of the edge made it hard going. Chase fought like hell with the freakish, octopus-type robot. The metal arms held him in place, though his arms and legs were free.

"Get me out of this fucking thing."

Wildly splashing, Rudolpho tried to reach the ledge and drag himself out. One of the small sharks latched onto the flowing material of his robe and tugged viciously at it.

Clawing against the tile, Duncan managed to find a finger hold in a small crack and desperately pulled himself up and out of the water. Reaching into the pocket of his jacket, he tried to pull out his Magno-Grappler Fighter Ray gun to free Chase as Nerk went rushing to his master's aid.

Hearing a loud ripping sound, Duncan looked down into the pool just in time to see a completely naked Rudolpho hanging on for dear life to Nerk. "Pull, you stupid moron! Pull!"

Chase gasped as the robot's arms fell to the sides, releasing him. A quick glance at the absurdity of Rudolpho's situation left Chase in stitches and when he looked back up from where he was doubled over, he caught a wink from Nerk.

Duncan laughed too hard to react at first. The sight of Rudolpho lying naked and gasping on the puke green tile was a once in a lifetime opportunity. When he could catch his breath, Duncan yelled, "Hey, Rudy, what the hell are you doing to this place?"

"The master is trying to build a resort," Nerk answered in all seriousness.

Chase just rolled his eyes and held up the coiled Cellular Biologic Warp Whip. "Wanna get kinky, baby?"

"Oh, that's nice, love." Giving the whip an appreciative look, Duncan had a few ideas for its use. "Last one back to the ship has to kiss Rudy next time around." No sooner were the words out than Duncan raced back toward their ship.

"Oh, fuck no!" Chase's shout rang out as he caught up with Duncan, slamming him into the hull opposite the door as the ship's ramp closed. Pressing close, he grinned.

"You lost, babe." Duncan smirked at him. Running his hands over the front of Chase's uniform, Duncan fiddled with getting him out of it. "I'm looking forward to seeing you lay one on Rudy next time."

Chase huffed and slapped Duncan's hip with the coiled whip. "I think not. But I do think I'd like to see you on your knees and my cock between those sweet lips of yours."

"Mmmhmm, I'd like to see that, too." A wicked grin spread across Duncan's lips when Chase got him with the whip. Letting go of him, Duncan backed away before turning to head to the main deck. After struggling out of the wet uniform, he dropped it to the ground and turned to face Chase, dropping to his knees.

Slapping the safety button on the door to keep it open, Chase braced himself in the doorway, grinning down at Duncan. When they both were finally naked, he held his cock out, stroking Duncan's lips with the head, slicking them.

"Come on, baby," he whispered gruffly, "open up for me."

Duncan's tongue licked and probed at the slit, tasting the slick juice. Resting his hands on the sides of Chase's legs, Duncan caressed his fingers over the skin. Opening his mouth, he took Chase fully in and his tongue slid along the shaft, teasing.

"Fuck yes." Chase's hips pushed forward, sliding his cock deeper into his navigator's mouth. "Love your mouth, baby. Love you."

Duncan nipped gently at the swollen flesh. One hand moved to Chase's balls, cupping beneath them and rolling them in his palm. Looking upward, Duncan drank in the intensity of desire flaring in Chase's expression.

Determined to hold Duncan's gaze, Chase thrust in and out, the movements quickening in time with his breathing. "Duncan..." He spread his legs and barely caught the door frame with his other hand before he was coming, shooting his load down Duncan's throat.

Duncan sucked harder, increasing the spasms. When the trembling of Chase's body stilled, Duncan cleaned him off, then settled back against his heels, flashing him a grin. "Take the edge off nicely for you, love?"

Chase chuckled as he worked to catch his breath. "Oh, yeah." He reached out, then realized the whip was still in his hand. Shaking his head, he laughed. "You needin', babe?"

"If we had time, I'd ask you to practice on me. I've heard those things can really send you into orbit." Duncan got off the floor and walked toward the navigator's chair. "I'd say you riding me wouldn't be amiss. If you're in the mood."

Quirking an eyebrow, Chase walked toward him, the whip falling to the floor. "If I'm in the mood?" He tugged open the console drawer and got out the lube. "Babe, the day I turn down the chance to have you inside me in any way possible, is the day you might as well commit my ass to the funny farm."

Settling in the chair, Duncan held his arms open for Chase. "I thought you'd say that." His cock stood at attention, waiting for its proper worship, and the wide grin remained plastered on his lips.

Chase smiled and popped the lube open as he straddled Duncan's thighs. "Get me ready, babe?" He held up the tube and grinned.

Taking it from him, Duncan squeezed a generous portion along his fingers. Then he tossed the tube and it landed near the console. Duncan lowered his hand between Chase's legs and pushed two fingers inside, rubbing against the inner gland to arouse Chase. Keeping his eyes on Chase, Duncan tipped his head back and his other hand pulled Chase's head toward him.

"Duncan." The navigator's name was breathed hot against his neck, Chase riding Duncan's fingers. "More, baby."

With his fingers wriggling gently inside Chase, Duncan let him enjoy it a moment longer before he pulled them out. With no more than a slight shift of his hips, his cock penetrated Chase's ass. Pulling down on Chase's hips, Duncan buried himself balls deep in the tight heat. He moaned and turned his head to catch Chase's lips with his own.

Chase dove into the kiss, tongue pushing into Duncan's mouth. The captain rode Duncan hard, rocking and grinding, fingers gripping Duncan's shoulders tightly.

Duncan thrust repeatedly and tremors began to build and race through him. He took hold of Chase's cock, already hard again, and timed every push with the fast rhythm of his hand. When Chase's muscles tightened around him, a jolt shot through Duncan and he pumped harder into Chase. His head fell back against his chair and with a shout, Duncan came.

Following right behind him, Chase gasped and groaned, hips jerking as he shot over Duncan's fist. When he was finally able to catch his breath, he dropped his head to Duncan's shoulder.

"Oh, damn... so fucking good, baby."

Before Duncan could say anything or even catch his breath, Arch's voice came over the com. "Lexerta Quadrant needs a delivery of Curing Toxic Diagnostician Bane ASAP. The shipment will be ready for pickup by the time you dock at Keyasa."

Lifting his head, Duncan groaned. "Fuck, Arch, you have the worst damn timing."

"Is that a Cellular Biologic Warp Whip I see? You guys have been antagonizing Rudolpho again, haven't you?" Without waiting for the obvious answer, Arch barked out, "On my desk when you get back. Deal with it, boys. Arch out."

Chase lifted an eyebrow but didn't move. "He sounds... stressed."

With a sigh, Duncan shifted. "Guess we're going to Keyasa. At least we can get a decent dinner there." He slapped Chase's ass, and they got dressed.

Chapter Fourteen

When they entered Rosetta's, the diner was half empty. Thankfully they were able to get one of the booths and had time to eat their dinner while the crew loaded the ship. Sitting across from Chase, Duncan rested his hand over Chase's and perused the menu.

"What looks good to you, babe?" Chase asked as he looked over his own menu.

Laying the menu to the side, Duncan shifted lower in his seat and his foot rubbed against the inside of Chase's leg. "I think just a steak and some fries."

Chase hummed softly, glancing up to give Duncan a smile. "Yeah, that does sound good."

When the waitress came to get their orders, Chase ordered for them both. She moved off back to the kitchen and he settled lower into the seat, content to play footsy.

"What the hell do you mean by that?" The sound of the voice in the booth behind Duncan began to rise in sharp agitation.

"You're taking this shit too seriously. You really are."

Duncan barely caught the low murmured answer when he turned his head to look back at the other two men.

"So much for your promises, Ike. So, who is it this time?" After the guy asked the question, he held up his hand to silence any sort of answer. "Oh, what the fuck do I care?"

Chase leaned to the side slightly, peering around Duncan. "Damn," he whispered.

Abruptly, one of the men, apparently Ike, stood without a word and stalked off, leaving the other guy staring after him, muttering, "Fucking bastard. I'm not going after you. I don't give a damn."

Seeing Chase's expression, Duncan twisted to try to get a better look at what held his husband's attention.

The mutters continued. "God damn it all to hell, you didn't pay for the meal. How am I supposed to pay for it?"

Without a word, Chase waved over the waitress. When she came up to the table, he lowered his voice. "How much was his meal? We'll pay it."

Obviously hearing Chase, the young man looked directly at both of them and Duncan got his first full look. Something about the pale, fragile features, surrounded by fiery red curls, gripped Duncan's full attention. The hauntingly mesmerizing, smoke-gray eyes stared into his for a brief moment. There was a hopeless, lost quality in those eyes and beyond that, something else tugged at Duncan.

"You need a bit of help, and we're happy to give it."

For a moment, the young man looked like he didn't know what to say. His anger dissolved into a more vulnerable expression. "He's an ass. But I've got no where else to go."

"Yes, you do," Chase said without hesitation. "Our ship is waiting at the dock."

Duncan didn't even question Chase's announcement. He just smiled reassuringly and proceeded to introduce them both. "I'm Duncan, and this rough-looking fellow is Chase. Why don't you come sit with us while you tell us your name?"

"I'm Eezy." Though he readily gave his name, he showed some hesitation in joining them. "Are you sure it's all right?"

"Yes, we are." Chase scooted over, flashing Duncan a grin. Then he patted the seat. "Come on, sit down."

Still eyeing both of them, Eezy slid out of his booth and stood. A few seconds later, he sat next to Chase. The waitress brought their food, setting their plates and drinks on the table. Looking at Eezy, she asked, "Want any dessert, hon?"

"Get anything you want. And bring him a coffee, too." Picking up his knife and fork, Duncan began cutting into his steak.

"I'll take a Tangy Cosmodots sundae. Thanks."

Chase glanced at Eezy out of the corner of his eye. "Want a bite?" He held up a forked piece of steak to Eezy, smiling gently.

Obviously Eezy hadn't eaten much since he showed no hesitation in leaning forward to take the meat. With a frown, Duncan grabbed for the waitress before she could leave. "Get him a steak and fries, then bring the sundae."

After he swallowed the piece, Eezy asked curiously, "You two do this often?"

"Do what?" Chase asked quietly, entranced by their new dinner guest.

"Take in people in trouble?"

Duncan started laughing with the question. "You could say that, Eezy. We're heading over to Lexerta Quadrant to deliver some supplies. We wouldn't mind you coming along for the ride if you want."

"I think..." Eezy looked at Duncan, then turned that mesmerizing gaze on Chase. "I think I'd like that," he said quietly.

Chase just swallowed, his meal forgotten.

The gentle prod of Duncan's foot nudged Chase's shin. A moment later the waitress returned and set Eezy's food in front of him. Before she could leave, Duncan said, "When we're done, bring all three of us TC sundaes."

"You got it, hon." After winking at Duncan, she turned on her heel to deal with another customer trying to get her attention.

"I really appreciate this," Eezy said quietly before he started on the steak.

"You're very welcome." Chase gave Duncan a look that was something between want and sheer need.

Smiling back at him, Duncan's hand covered Chase's with a gentle squeeze. They were both definitely affected by the vibrant young man at their table. To keep things casual, Duncan addressed Chase. "It shouldn't take us too long to drop off those supplies. Where you wanna head for our day off?"

Chase nodded. "Yeah. Yeah, that sounds good." He let out a slow breath and looked back over at Eezy. Just being near the young man was almost a magical experience.

Looking up, Eezy said in-between bites, "Are you guys... together?"

"We're married." Duncan answered before he eyed Chase. "You didn't answer my question, babe."

Eezy demolished his steak before they finished theirs and the waitress brought their desserts and took their plates when they'd finished.

Shaking his head, Chase blinked up at Duncan. "Oh, umm... home?"

"Yeah, we can do that. A peaceful, quiet day for the three of us." Digging into the ice cream, Duncan brought the spoon to his lips and licked it.

Eezy's gaze switched back and forth between the two of them, watching them quite avidly.

Chase stared at Duncan, watching intently. "Is it time to leave yet?" he grumbled quietly, shifting in the seat.

Grinning wickedly at him, Duncan asked, "Problems, love?" When the waitress returned with their check, Duncan gave her his card. "Add ten creds for yourself."

Giving him a pleased smile, the waitress slid his card over her pad, then returned it to him.

Standing, Duncan leaned toward Eezy, murmuring, "Don't mind Chase. He gets these moods."

Chase snorted and once he and Eezy were out of the booth, he reached for Duncan, giving him a deep, hungry kiss right there in the middle of the diner. "Home."

Duncan couldn't answer him verbally, instead his hand pressed against Chase's head, drawing him back into another kiss. For the moment, he wasn't aware of anything else around them but the taste of Chase's mouth. When he drew his head back, he caught Eezy staring at them. Chuckling, Duncan winked.

"Get used to it. We never get any better." With another laugh, he slid his arm around Chase's waist and headed for their ship.

Eezy fell into step behind them. "You two really act like you're in love," he said offhandedly.

"We are." Chase smiled at Duncan. "Very much so."

"How did you meet?"

"I'll let him tell that story since I told it last time." Duncan smirked and his arm tightened around Chase. Outside the diner, they headed toward the back docking bay farther down the street.

"We were both taking some time off, working for Interferion," Chase explained. "I ducked into some dive of a bar in an off world station with the intent on spending the weekend getting laid and drinking." He slipped an around Duncan's waist. "That weekend turned into years."

"A match made in a hellhole of a bar." Duncan winked at Eezy.

When they reached the ship, one of the crew members approached Chase and handed him the inventory pad. "It's all ready, Captain Sykes. They're expecting you in the LQ at 1700 hours."

Leaving Chase to sign, Duncan led Eezy into the ship. "You can have my cabin for the duration since I bunk with Chase."

Eezy looked around and grinned at Duncan. "Nice ship."

Chase boarded behind them, pressing the button to close the door. "You gonna show him around, babe?" he asked as he started for the bridge.

"Yeah, I'll show him to his quarters and let him get settled." Moving toward the back section of the ship, Duncan continued showing Eezy around. "You can go wherever you want, and the galley is right in there whenever you're hungry."

"I'm not sure how long I'll be staying with you guys, but I'm grateful for the place to stay."

Duncan leveled a serious look on him. "It's not really a problem. No reason to have to hang around the guy who ditched you, Eezy. You'll find better company here."

Opening the door to his cabin, Duncan walked in and stepped to the side for Eezy. The young man followed him and gave the cabin a once-over, nodding. Then he turned to face Duncan and smiled.

Finding himself the subject of that incredible gray, stormy gaze, Duncan stilled. "That guy is seriously an ass. I can't see how he'd just walk out on you."

Duncan couldn't resist moving closer and lifting his hand to Eezy's face. The smooth, flawless skin was warm beneath the tips of his fingers. Smiling slowly, Duncan's gaze fastened on the delicate line of Eezy's lips.

"And if I were to say that I'm glad he did?" Eezy closed the distance between them. The kiss began as a chaste one, just the slightest brush of their mouths to one another.

Allowing Eezy to guide him in what he wanted, Duncan's lips clung to the heat before parting slowly. The tip of Duncan's tongue darted briefly over them, waiting to see if Eezy would open to him. One hand lifted to the back of Eezy's head, gently pressing against him. A soft sound filled the kiss and Eezy dove right in, tongue sweeping through Duncan's mouth. Gone was the timid young man. Eezy showed nothing in the way of shy as he pressed up against Duncan's body, kissing him deeply.

Chapter Fifteen

Duncan stood in front of the shipment of Bane, listening to Chase talk to a member of the Keyasa crew.

"We're not sure how far the disease has progressed. CI added a regenerative enzyme to the cloud released on Lexerta."

"So CI's responsible for the contamination, Ternes?" Chase asked quietly before he glanced briefly at Duncan.

Duncan's brow rose, but he didn't say anything. He wasn't quite so sure he was buying much when it came to CI and Interferion announcements.

"That's the word on the byways. You don't have much time to get the Bane to Lexerta. I wish you guys luck. We've still got communication with them, but it's spotty at best. The planet is on alert and docking is prohibited. Commander Burton is waiting to give you the transport code to get to the surface."

"Thanks, Ternes. We'll be ready to go as soon as we talk to Burton."

"Better you than me on this one." Ternes eyed both of them before he turned to head out of the ship.

When Ternes left the bay, Duncan and Chase both looked at each other. Duncan was the first to speak and his tone was sarcastic. "CI up to his old tricks?"

"I've got the same feeling, babe. Nothing ever seems quite right when it comes to the big bosses and him."

"Let's talk to Burton and get out of here."

Leaving the ship, they walked across the huge docking bay to the back offices. Burton's office was the largest of the block at the end of a long corridor. Without knocking, Duncan walked in and Chase followed him.

"Hello, boys." Burton heartily greeted them. "You almost ready to leave?"

"The Bane is on the ship and Ternes filled us in. We just need the transport code."

"Very good, very good." Burton handed them a slender silver disc. "The Nav Com signal is on that. Also, I want you two to take this black case. As soon as you're done on Lexerta, I want you to take this to Alpha Ten."

When Burton pushed the large case toward them, Duncan picked it up. "Req form?"

"Nah, just a personal delivery to the substation. Just give it to Commander Carson for me."

Both of them nodded before they withdrew from the office. Nothing was said as they walked back down the long hall and across the mammoth docking bay. Once they were safely back on their ship, Duncan set the case down. Sitting in his chair, he studied the case for a long moment before he started typing in the navigation orders.

"You know, normally I wouldn't be so leery and seeing conspiracy behind every black leather case, but lately I am, Chase."

"I'm not about to ignore the odd feelings I've been getting lately either." Leaning over, Chase picked up the case.

"We ready to go, guys?" Eezy entered the deck and headed for his own chair beside Duncan's.

"Shipment is on board and we're heading for Lexerta now, Eezy. We're going to transport the Bane ourselves. So I'm volunteering you to help me with it." Duncan stopped for a moment to flash Eezy a wicked grin.

"So what am I supposed to do?" Eezy asked.

Chase chuckled and guided the ship out of the docking bay. "Just hang on for the ride."

After slipping in the transport code disc, Duncan settled back and grabbed the case from Chase. "Hmm, it's sealed. I'm damn curious as to what's inside. No req form, just a personal delivery. Seems sort of odd to me."

Eezy eyed the case, then Duncan and Chase. "What's going on?"

"We're not sure," Chase answered, staring at the case. "But things aren't adding up lately."

"Like what?"

"Like Burton wanting a personal delivery in the first place. Call me suspicious, but I can't help wondering since I know the station has had a problem with missing crystals. And then then nonsense about CI being behind the outbreak on Lexerta?" Duncan shook his head. "Everything is making me extremely uneasy lately." Duncan's nails tapped on the edge of the case as he studied the seal. "Shouldn't be hard at all for me to reprogram this thing after I take a look inside."

"CI?"

Chase grinned at Duncan. "Go for it, love." Looking at Eezy, then Duncan, he said, "Interferion's 'supposed' number one enemy."

"What's so bad about him?" Eezy asked quietly.

Running one nail slowly beneath the seal, Duncan popped the connection to the latch. Opening the case, the distinct blue glow of the crystals gave away exactly what was inside.

"Well, apparently CI loves to steal these." Turning the case, Duncan showed them the crystals. "And either Commander Burton is in league with CI and he'll be somewhere nearby when we reach Alpha Ten, or something else is going on. It's been reported that these crystals were already stolen by CI. What do you make of it, love?"

Eezy just stared at the crystals for a long moment. "Those things are worth a fortune in creds, aren't they?"

Chase was silent for a moment. Then he nodded. "Yeah, they are, Eezy." He looked up at Duncan. "You sure there are only two missing?"

Duncan nodded to Chase. "I'm really starting to get pissed because so much isn't adding up lately. What happened to the good old days of knowing who our enemy was? I'm willing to bet either Burton is in this for personal gain, or there just happens to be some conveniently missing crystals to blame on CI. I say we do a little investigation while we're on Lexerta. I'd lay good money it isn't CI behind the outbreak. Only thing is, I'm afraid of who might be."

Solemnly quiet, Eezy didn't seem to know what to say and it took him a moment to speak. "It sounds like you guys are in some serious shit."

Nodding, Chase asked, "Eezy, you ever been in a situation where you begin to think that you're on the wrong side of things? When you've been told, trained even, to believe a particular person is your enemy, only to find clues later that toss that theory on its head?"

"Yeah, I know the feeling very well." The sarcasm in Eezy's statement was easily heard but hard to define, and both Duncan and Chase glanced at him.

"Lexerta in range, guys. Happy healing." Mal's cheerful voice interrupted their conversation.

Duncan leaned forward to flip on the com switch. "Lexerta, Interferion 212 ready to transport. Acknowledge."

A moment of silence followed and Duncan repeated the message again.

Still no response.

Chase sat rigid in his seat, expression grim. "Duncan... something's not right here."

Opening the armory tray, Duncan nodded. "Ternes said communication was spotty. It could be that, but just in case, we arm up." After selecting a few weapons for himself, Duncan picked out one for Eezy and tossed it over to him.

Eezy caught the taser, giving Duncan and Chase both a wry look. "You two get into this sort of thing often?"

"Nah," Chase said as he shoved his own taser into the holster on his belt. "We just like to be prepared."

"He's lying. It's our hobby. Really." Laughing, Duncan stood and led the way to the transport platform. Chase grabbed the cases of Bane and joined them. Without saying a word, Duncan activated the equipment. A momentary haze settled over them, then cleared abruptly, leaving them standing in the docking bay of Lexerta. An ominous quiet greeted them.

"This place should be a hive right about now." Frowning, Duncan drew his gun before he stepped off the platform.

The sound of a distant rumble seemed to come from outside the building and Duncan cautiously approached the outer door. Opening it to look out, chaos greeted him.

"What the fuck...?" Chase stood behind him, tense immediately. "Oh, my God..."

"Umm, guys?" Eezy said quietly, standing near them.

"Fuck, the infection's reached critical already. We've got to set off the Bane." Before Duncan could react, two zombies next to a nearby dumpster started toward them. Before Duncan or Chase could get a shot off, Eezy drew his Neuron Pulser and fired damn near point blank at both of the creatures. Chase stumbled backward, too stunned at Eezy's quickness to do much of anything.

Eezy held out a hand for the case. "Let's get this done and get the fuck out of here."

"We've got to get to the roof! It's the only chance!" The sounds of the horrific screams of people under attack surrounded them and when Duncan tried to shut the door, it was wrenched out of his hand.

As the trio scrambled back from their position, several creatures flooded into the bay. Drool and pus wet their pale green features and the drone of their sounds began to rise to a deafening level. Clearly the disease had reached its critical stage, and deformities within the living tissue of the bodies had already killed off a good portion of normal cells. Grotesque lesions covered the bodies of the victims in varying states of advanced decay. They were literally being driven mad by the rapid decomposition.

"Fuck!" Chase grabbed Eezy and Duncan, tugging them toward one of the stairwells leading to the second floor. "Move it!"

Although they were slow and clumsy, the zombies inched toward them, closing the distance. Chase took the stairs two at a time, Duncan and Eezy right on his heels just as a rotting arm reached up between the metal steps. When they got to the top, Chase ran down the catwalk toward the doorway leading up to the roof. Eezy and Duncan were behind him, shooting at the bodies crowding the stairs and struggling to climb them. Crouching at the railing, Duncan aimed and took out several of the zombies. Eezy stood beside him, firing into the rising tide of bodies.

"Get to the roof, Chase, and set that damn thing off! We'll hold 'em back from here!"

Chase shoved the door open and ran out, dropping to his knees. He opened the case and set the timer. No sooner than he made it back to the door, a beam of pulsing blue light shot into the sky. Seconds later, the vaporous cloud spread out. Chase coughed and spluttered, stumbling back down the steps to Duncan and Eezy.

Chapter Sixteen

The situation had a desperate edge as Eezy and Duncan kept firing at the demented creatures. Uncertain how long it would be before the Bane took effect, Duncan racked his brain for a way out.

The floor below them was crawling with infected citizens. Unfortunately, they blocked the way to the transport platform. The clamor rose to a near unbearable level, making it impossible for Duncan to use his com link.

"There's too fucking many of them to stay here. We're going to have to hole up in one of the back offices until this shit takes effect." As he spoke, Duncan pointed toward one of the doors at the back of the bay. Since the people were milling at the bottom of the staircase, none were in the way of getting to the bay offices.

"We should be able to get through to headquarters, too. They need to send the med teams in here. We can't keep shooting these guys." Chase pulled out a line wire and quickly ran it along the surface of the railing near them. A second later it fused to the metal and a barbed end propelled forward, embedding in the wall above the back hall to the offices.

After expertly picking off several of the creatures coming up the stairs, Duncan looked over at both of them. "I'll keep their attention here while you two get down there. It'll buy a bit of time before they notice anything."

Eezy took shots at a couple of the people trying to get up the second set of stairs near the compound lifter. Already a number of them had gotten to the third level walk-ways. Chase frowned at Duncan, and Duncan scowled at him.

"Go ahead. I'll be right behind you once you guys get in."

They really didn't have much of a choice, and none of them could afford the damn creatures blocking off access to the offices. Chase grabbed Eezy by the shoulders and pulled him up. "You go first."

"Fuck!" Duncan fired a quick shot and picked off a woman who had crept up behind Chase. "Go, Eezy. Hurry up!"

Chase whirled and started firing down the catwalk at three zombies who had broken through. Eezy quickly scrambled over the railing and attached a holder to the wire before he went over the edge, flying through the air.

None of them were shooting to kill; they were doing their damnedest only to disable. Minute signs of the Bane's effect were already starting to show in the slowing movements. The drug had begun to take hold on the disease and slow its progression in the systems of the infected inhabitants.

When Eezy landed, Duncan pushed Chase toward the wire. "Go ahead, love. I expect to see the med teams there when I join you guys."

Chase nodded as he climbed over the railing. Left to deal with the advancing creatures, Duncan dropped four of them while Chase slid down the line wire. They were getting too close, and Duncan didn't have much time himself. Even though it was clear the Bane was working, the ravages of the disease left on some of the victims were horrific. They needed the med teams down there immediately.

Looking down, Duncan saw Chase had landed safely. With the other two in the clear, Duncan moved toward the line wire to make his own escape. He didn't even spare any time to take out the rest of the people swarming up the stairs and catwalk. Attaching the holder to the wire, Duncan pushed off. Abruptly, he was left dangling in mid-air when a strong hand grabbed him by the throat. Any sound he made was cut off as the hand squeezed tightly and tried to pull him back. Clawing at the fingers around his throat, Duncan's other hand held to the metal holder.

The sound of a loud pop near his ear was followed by an easing of the pressure around his neck. He only had time to look down and see Chase gesturing frantically and Eezy aiming for another shot before he flew through the air down the wire. Landing with less than his usual grace, Duncan scrambled into the com room, pushing Chase and Eezy ahead of him. With a loud clang, he slammed the door shut behind them.

Immediately, Duncan moved for the com board. Thankfully, it hadn't been damaged and he hastily sent out a message on their status, and the three of them dealt with the frantic reports coming in from both the interplanetary com and Interferion.

* * *

Entering the cabin, Duncan saw Chase already relaxing on the bed and Eezy emerging from the shower cylinder.

"Just got the report from the med teams on Lexerta. They finally got everything under control. The casualty total is nearing two thousand, but it shouldn't go much higher than that." Duncan flopped onto the edge of the bed, sliding his jacket and his shirt off.

"Sounds like we made it there just in time," Eezy murmured near Duncan's ear as he leaned in to nuzzle against his throat.

Closing his eyes, Duncan tipped his head slightly. Chase reached over, running his hand slowly downward over Duncan's bare chest.

"We earned a bit of R and R," Chase said.

Duncan wasn't about to argue with the captain's decision. The press of Chase's hand pushed him backward to the bed and Eezy knelt, hovering over Duncan. Both Eezy and Chase were already naked and hands quickly divested Duncan of the rest of his uniform.

Eezy homed in on the side of Duncan's throat and Chase lavished his own attention on the other side. For several long moments, only the sound of their quickening breathing accompanied the stray caresses of hands over silky flesh. With a growl, Duncan shifted their position, rolling Eezy to his back and quickly straddling him. Staring in the smoky eyes pinned on him, Duncan could feel their pull. He could feel himself getting lost in the all-encompassing intensity. When he turned his head to look back at Chase, the same feeling held him imprisoned as he stared at his husband. They both knew what was happening. A current of complete understanding ran between them in that moment.

Capturing Eezy's hands, Duncan held them above his head. As he leaned down to kiss Eezy, Chase moved behind Duncan. The massage of his hands ran intimately along the length of Duncan's body and drew an incoherent sound of need from the navigator. The inward press of his thumbs slid along the crack of Duncan's ass, causing his hips to grind more tightly against Eezy beneath him.

Eezy freed his hands long enough to grab for one of the tubes always kept near at hand. After coating his hand with the gel, he wrapped his fingers around Duncan's cock, smoothing the clear liquid over the hardened flesh. The next moment, Chase's slicked fingers entered Duncan and the movement of Duncan's hips rocked between the exquisite sensations.

"You're both trying to make me lose it," Duncan muttered as he opened his eyes and saw Eezy grinning at him with an unholy glee. The look faltered when Duncan's fingers lightly trailed over the head of Eezy's cock before trapping it against a harder grind of his hips.

"That's the idea," Chase whispered, fingers spreading Duncan open. "How do you want him, Eezy?"

Lust-glazed eyes held Duncan's for a moment and the slight rise of Eezy's hips answered Chase. "I want you in me and I want to be inside him," Eezy said. Duncan closed his eyes, his moan of agreement the only thing he could manage.

"Mmm, scoot that sweet ass up, babe." Helping to position Duncan, Chase groaned as he watched Eezy's long, slender cock slide deep into his husband's body. "Oh, God..."

Eezy hissed, hands landing on Duncan's hips as he rocked upward. "Fuck, you feel good."

The press of Duncan's hips encouraged the torturously slow friction inside his ass. Leaning over, both of his hands rested on Eezy's chest when one particular thrust grazed deep inside him.

"Let me in, gorgeous," Chase coaxed softly. Eezy's eyes rolled back as Chase pushed two fingers inside him. "Lord, you're tight..."

"Been... a while..." Eezy exhaled. Eyes opening, he stared up into Duncan's, words no longer needed between them.

One of Duncan's hands reached for Chase as he slowly rode Eezy's cock. The smallest movement constricted around Eezy, sending jolts of increasing tension through both of them. Duncan's fingers curled against Chase for balance as he leaned back toward his husband, needing to feel the solid body behind him. Turning his head slightly, he whispered, "Love you, babe."

With one look at Chase, Duncan knew he wanted the same thing. They both wanted Eezy as a more permanent fixture with them. As he slid deep into Eezy, Chase licked Duncan's lips.

"Love you," Chase whispered, thrusting into Eezy's body.

"Chase!" Eezy bucked, driving his own cock hard into Duncan.

"Oh, fuck." Duncan shuddered against them, his head tipping back toward Chase. The grind of his body became more frantic and his fingers clawed at Eezy with the stronger pulses flooding him.

Taking a harder hold on Duncan's hips, Eezy fucked him with a jarring strength. Each time he withdrew slightly, his ass ground tighter to Chase.

"Need you," Chase breathed into Duncan's ear, his own thrusts turning hard and quick as he dove repeatedly into Eezy. "Need him."

Later they would talk, but, for the moment, all thought was driven out by the intensity riding Duncan. His hand quickly wrapped around his cock and the sensations sent his mind reeling as he came hard. Trapped by both of them, Eezy quickly followed and the spasms of his body signaled his own release.

"Oh, sweet fuck..." Chase jerked, shouting as he came hard and fast, hips slamming into Eezy. Dazed and breathless, and more than a touch out of it, he eased out of Eezy slowly, turning to collapse onto the bed beside their companion.

"Damn," Eezy panted. "That was... intense."

Collapsing on Eezy, Duncan tried to catch his breath. One hand remained on Chase and the other caressed Eezy. He didn't say anything right away; he really couldn't. When Eezy's hand smoothed over his hair, Duncan turned his head slightly to press a soft kiss to Eezy's palm. The tip of Eezy's finger traced over his lips, making him smile. Only time would tell if Eezy wanted to stay, but Duncan realized he'd do his damnedest to try to get him to.

Episode Five: Do We Know What's Going On?

Chapter Seventeen

"Release the super-fast, crazed mechanical alligators that feed off fear!" Rudolpho waved his arms wildly at Nerk. "Open the portal, you fool!"

Duncan tried to grab Nerk but just missed as the assistant bolted passed him. With Chase nowhere to be seen, Duncan sprinted for the metal stairs and sat down on the upper step to await the inevitable.

As several fifteen-foot alligators emerged from the portal, they milled about the floor aimlessly. Frustrated, Rudolpho began screeching at them. "He's over there, you stupid creatures! Get him!"

The alligators appeared to be extremely disinterested in Duncan and completely ignored Rudolpho. Three of them began to move toward one of the vats of sea water as the others explored their new surroundings.

Duncan came close to bursting out laughing. Cytelsian alligators wouldn't attack anything unless they could smell fear. Rudolpho's rage and Duncan's amusement were nowhere near that state. Nerk, Rudolpho's ever suffering protégé, stood near the portal key as Rudolpho advanced on him, shouting at the top of his lungs. "Nerk, you imbecile, recalibrate the portal!"

Before Nerk could move, Chase careened around some stacked crates and barreled straight into Rudolpho. Reacting in a split second, Duncan launched a line wire, snagging Chase's uniform just as Rudolpho fell backward over the railing and down to the ground.

Landing in the midst of the alligators, it took Rudolph a moment to realize exactly where he was. A terrified shriek filled the room and the alligators went immediately for Rudolpho. With the creatures occupied, Chase untangled himself from the cord.

Rudolpho jumped on top of a contam barrel before any of the reptiles could bite him. The alligators began congregating around the barrel, vicious teeth snapping at the air.

"Ready to go?" Duncan eyed Chase, waiting for him as Rudolpho began cursing up a blue streak. Nerk's ancestry and intelligence were called into question, in no uncertain terms, as the poor Riseon worked frantically to get the alligators away from Rudolpho and back into the portal.

Grinning at Duncan, Chase jumped over the railing to join him. "Should we help him out? It won't take those guys long to chew through ol' Rudy's Deflect Barrier."

Glancing between the still-screaming Rudolpho and Nerk doing his best to corral the enormous beasts, Duncan sighed. "Suppose we should, shouldn't we?"

"You take the two on the left, and I'll get the other three."

Simultaneously they pulled out their Penetrating Blackout-Units and began firing at their targets. A moment later the smell of singed amphibian flesh and blessed silence filled the room.

"At least Rudy shut up." Holstering his gun, Duncan high-fived Chase before they turned to leave the warehouse. Just as they reached the exit, Rudolpho started yelling once again at Nerk, who was trying to drag the stunned alligators back into the portal.

"Nerk, I'll leave you to the Psionic Pepper Dragon of the Astral Plane if you don't…"

Duncan slammed the door behind them, cutting off Rudolpho's haranguing of his grossly underpaid and overworked servant.

Making their way back into the ship, they settled on the bridge and prepared to leave the planet. Chase relaxed in his seat, waving a Beacon-Darkon Darkener at Duncan. "Better than what I said I would get."

"Damn, babe, I thought you were only going to go for the Cremator Blaster."

"Our skills are slipping. I didn't even know he had this damned thing." Lightly patting the blue-green nanosteel rod embedded in the black steel, Chase smirked at him.

"Market will have several bidders, or maybe we should keep that baby for ourselves."

"My desk is a better place." Without so much as a hello, Arch's voice cut into their conversation. "I want you two at main headquarters. Assignment top priority, not to be discussed until you meet with Commander Zantex. Arch out."

"Ya know, he always says that but never says a thing when it doesn't show up on his desk." Laughing, Duncan reached for Chase.

When Eezy entered, he eyed the two as Chase climbed into Duncan's lap. "I take it aggravating Rudolpho and your boss are normal occurrences for you two."

"Pretty much." Duncan held out a hand to Eezy then pulled him toward them. "Why don't you undress and save me the trouble?"

"Lazy," Eezy teased as he unzipped his pants and shoved them down one-handed.

"Not for long." Duncan released his hand and lowered it to encircle Eezy's cock. Chase squirmed in Duncan's lap, shrugging out of his uniform while Eezy finished undressing. A soft groan escaped Eezy, his hips nudging into Duncan's hand.

"You need to undress, love," Chase murmured in Duncan's ear before he pressed a light kiss to the side of his throat. One hand moved between them, kneading the front of Duncan's pants.

After Chase climbed off of Duncan's lap, they both began undressing the navigator and all of their clothing ended up in a heap on the floor. Chase opened one of the small drawers on the console and pulled out a tube. Squeezing a generous amount into his hand, he leaned down to slick Duncan's cock as Duncan hungrily kissed him. A moment later, Chase grabbed Eezy's arm then pushed him down onto Duncan's lap.

Duncan positioned his cock and Eezy lowered his ass onto it, letting it stretch and fill him. Eezy's hand covered his own cock, beginning a tantalizing rhythm with the pull of his hand. None of them said anything and only the softer sounds of their groans of pleasure disrupted the quiet.

As Chase watched, he played with himself. "Fuck him, babe. I want to see you fuck him hard."

The movement of Eezy's hips quickened in response to the words and rising need engulfed both of them. Duncan's hand moved to Chase's hip and drew him closer. Turning his head, he opened his mouth to take in Chase's cock. A low murmur of appreciation vibrated over the length as Duncan swallowed .

Eezy's hand joined Duncan's, and together they caressed Chase and each other, running over flesh and entangling in hair. All three of them were intent in their own world of sensations. The friction of Eezy's ass tightening around him had Duncan fucking him harder, each thrust followed by a low grunt of sound as he sucked Chase's cock.

"You two are too much." Eezy groaned, enrapt in the sight of the other two men and the feel of Duncan taking him over and over again.

Chase lowered his head and silenced Eezy in a hard kiss until Eezy had to pull back to drag in a ragged breath. Duncan's mouth and tongue worked over Chase, manipulating the hard flesh. In answer, Chase began to fuck his mouth in earnest.

The jerk of Eezy's hand ran quickly over his own cock until Duncan took over. A harsh groan escaped Eezy and he rocked tightly against Duncan. He shouted as he came, heat spilling over Duncan's hand.

With the contraction of muscles around him, Duncan strained upward into Eezy's ass as he shuddered. With a sharp cry, Chase came at the same time, filling Duncan's mouth. For several moments after, the three of them were locked together in their own private world of intense pleasure.

After cleaning off Chase's cock, Duncan pulled back his head and relaxed limply in the chair as Eezy and Chase cleaned off his hand. The feel of their tongues glided over his skin sent small shivers through him.

"We need to get ready for our headquarters visit," Duncan murmured.

"Yeah, I know." Chase rested his head on Duncan's shoulder, sighing.

"You want me to go along or stay behind?" Pressing a kiss to Duncan's hand, Eezy released it. Bending down, he picked up his clothes and started dressing.

"You can go with Chase. I'm going to see if I can't get a little information." Running his hand lightly over Chase's hair, Duncan added, "If he asks, tell Zantex I'm requisitioning supplies for the ship."

Chase chuckled. "Just don't get caught, love."

"You know better than that." Duncan slapped Chase's ass. "Now get dressed."

Chapter Eighteen

"You two go ahead and talk to the brass." Duncan settled in his chair and pulled up the main com screen.

"Be careful, babe." Chase watched him for a moment, then took Eezy's arm and began walking toward the ship's exit.

Maneuvering their way through the maze that was headquarters, Chase and Eezy took the elevator to the tenth floor of the glass and nanosteel compound. Clearly a great deal more money had been spent on the décor of the Interferion home. Massive murals from the likes of Dante and Sam Estes lined the corridor they walked down. Most of the doors were shut, but Chase knew they opened onto the luxurious offices of Interferion's top brass.

Eyeing a frieze done for the Battle of Ursona, Chase smirked. "Nice to know that costs more than I get paid in ten years."

"This place is like a museum." Eezy muttered, shaking his head in wonder.

Pausing in front of the door to Zantex's office, Chase rested his hand on the doorknob. "You ready to be properly impressed?"

"I'm sure I will be," Eezy remarked dryly.

Opening the door, Chase stepped inside and went to the clerk's desk. "We're here to see Commander Zantex."

The young Zytrues looked up at Chase and nodded. "She's been waiting for you. Go ahead."

Chase rested his hands on the desk, leaning forward. "Any hints on the hush project, Tanu?"

"Not this time, Chase. No files have crossed my desk on whatever is going on." Grinning at him, she added, "You can fill me in when you guys take me to lunch."

"For the lack of information, it's good only for a cheese sandwich."

"I'm ordering Vela steak anyway."

"I'll think about it." Laughing, Chase straightened and headed toward the closed door behind Tanu.

When Chase opened the door and went inside, Eezy followed him silently. In the inner office, the first thing Chase noticed was the man standing near Zantex's desk. Silvery-white hair flowed over his shoulders like water, covering a flawless athletic physique.

"We've been waiting for you, Sykes." Completely ignoring Eezy, Zantex gestured toward the stranger. "This is Astrasur, demon lord of the H-37 dimension."

As Astrasur turned his head to look at them, piercing golden eyes captured Chase's and sent a shiver down his spine. Arch had seriously outdone himself sending them on this mission, whatever it might be. Answering the regal nod of the demon's head with one of his own, Chase took his own sweet time looking over Astrasur. The demon lord was dressed in black, shimmering kalarir. The outfit clung to every gorgeous line and ripple of muscle.

Chase's gaze went to the ruby red lips and he smiled faintly, watching the tip of Astrasur's tongue wet those lips. Eezy stood beside him in his own trance, staring at the demon lord.

"Pleasure," Chase murmured as he moved toward the Commander's desk. Turning to look at Zantex, Chase saw the roll of the woman's eyes and the compression of her lips.

"Now that I have your attention, Sykes," Zantex's tone held an extremely sarcastic note. "We can get on with business. Lord Astrasur is here to negotiate a trade treaty with Brenth. You will be escorting him."

"Yes, ma'am," Chase said, doing his damnedest to keep his eyes on Zantex and not the tall piece of work near him. "We've taken on a new crew member." He turned and took Eezy's hand, tugging him closer.

"Eezy, this is Commander Zantex. Commander, this is Eezy. He's our..." He paused for a moment and glanced over at Eezy, who was too busy biting back a chuckle to help. "Our morale officer."

One of Zantex's eyebrows rose. "I see," she said dryly. "Welcome to the nuthouse, Eezy."

"Thank you, Commander." Eezy squeezed Chase's hand slightly. "It's been... an experience."

"Yes." Zantex cleared her throat. "As I said, you will be escorting Lord Astrasur. And boys, don't fuck this up."

Chase's grin was utterly unrepentant. "Why, Commander, have we ever let you down?"

"No, but I keep waiting for you to," Zantex retorted sarcastically before she turned her attention back to Astrasur. "Captain Sykes will make sure your journey is uneventful."

As Astrasur looked over at Chase, an appreciative smirk flit over his lips. "I am sure he will."

Directing one of her infamous 'no nonsense' gazes at Chase, Zantex added, "Won't you, Chase?"

Eezy eyed the three of them, his best innocent expression firmly plastered on his face. Chase's attempt wasn't even close; his grin simply widened.

"Get out of here," Zantex grumbled, waving them off.

Giving the Commander a mock salute and Astrasur a teasing wink, Chase said, "Your chariot awaits."

Eezy laughed and went out first, shaking his head. "It's no wonder you two are so well-known throughout the galaxy."

"Hey, what can I say?" Chase draped an arm over Eezy's shoulders as Astrasur fell in beside them. "We do our best."

Zantex didn't even bother commenting as the three of them left the office. Chase's arm tightened around Eezy before it dropped away.

"What about my steak, Chase?" Before Chase could escape the office, the clerk tried to get his attention.

"Can't this time. Next time around, Tanu, I promise."

"Expect a bill on your cred account." Tanu winked at him then went back to work.

* * *

After getting Astrasur comfortable, Chase joined Eezy and Duncan on the bridge. As he sat in his chair, he noticed the fierce concentration etched on his husband's features. "Is it that good?"

"Shit, babe. You aren't going to believe this." Duncan's fingers flew rapidly over the key pad, bringing up screen after screen.

Eezy moved toward Duncan, settling on the arm of his chair and resting his hand on the navigator's shoulder. "What is it?"

Duncan shook his head. "Some fucked up shit, that's for sure. I've been going through old Interferion records—stuff that hasn't seen the light of day in ages—and you won't believe the dirt I've found. Nobody understands that even when they delete their memos, they can still be accessed. Morons."

"Okay..." Chase moved closer. "So, what's the deal? What have you found?"

Duncan looked up at Eezy, then Chase. "They murdered CI's father."

Both of them stared back at Duncan, stunned. A moment later Chase found his voice. "For what reason? They had a treaty with Usilusis and Brenth."

"Yeah, but not like the one they have with his successor Oera. Not only did they kill Usilusis, but the bullshit they laid on CI made certain CI wouldn't inherit his father's crown. And it went to Oera."

"You sure about all of that?" Eezy asked with an odd intensity.

Glancing over at him, Duncan nodded. "It's in the records. The man who assassinated Usilusis was never caught. I found the records of a certain Ensign Drake Collins and he spilled the beans. The account was taken off the database, but not before a group from the underground got a hold of it."

Eezy shook his head and dropped back into his own seat. "What could they gain from it?"

Chase sighed and sat down as well. "A lot, I would imagine. CI comes from a very wealthy family, with a military force that rivals most other factions. The chance to get their hands on it would have been too strong to pass up."

"So it was merely political? Military?"

"Isn't it always?" Duncan asked. He twisted his chair around until he was facing Chase and Eezy.

Eezy nodded slowly. "I guess. Just never expected... I mean, it's just hard to believe that someone as strong as Usilusis could be overthrown so easily."

"What I find hard to believe is why CI wasn't outright killed as well," Chase muttered. "He was next in line, and certainly the strongest leader this world has seen in a very long time."

"Drake was designated as a three-two crim, but he disappeared before Interferion could arrest his ass. I also found an internal memo from Interferion President Xere to Commander Grant outlining the chances of CI signing the treaty they wanted with Brenth. The memo referred to the most likely successor that would sign as Oera. They wanted a treaty that gave Interferion complete control over Brenth. They didn't want a strong leader; they wanted an Interferion figure head." Sighing, Duncan shut off the screen. "I could hazard a guess they might have tried to kill CI, but obviously they failed and decided to set him up instead so he wouldn't inherit."

"How much do the crystals have to do with it?" Chase asked quietly.

"Probably the strongest factor of all, I'd say."

"You two seem to get into the deepest shit." Eezy smiled but it seemed a wan effort.

With a bit of concern, Chase laid his hand on Eezy's. "You're not in the middle of it, Eezy. Whatever we do, you won't get caught in the crossfire."

For the briefest moment, Eezy's eyes looked a touch haunted, but then it faded. "I know," he said finally.

Duncan leaned back in his seat, one foot propped on Chase's thigh. "All goes back to the 'working for the wrong people' if you ask me."

Eezy looked from Duncan to Chase. "What do you two think about CI? Honestly?"

Meeting Chase's gaze, Duncan nodded. "Yeah, and what do we do about it?"

"CI? That's a complicated question to answer, Eezy." Chase spoke for both of them. "We already knew he wasn't the enemy Interferion portrayed him as."

"We've meet him before. He's..." Trailing off, Duncan tried to find the words.

"You're the lucky SOB who kissed him." Chase smirked at Duncan.

Eezy bit his lip and grinned. "You kissed him? Did you enjoy it?"

Duncan laughed. "Enjoy it? Hell, I nearly creamed my pants!"

Chase rolled his eyes. "And all I got was the second-hand details."

"Aww..." Eezy slid out of his seat and straddled Chase's lap. "Poor thing," he whispered across the captain's lips.

"Yeah... poor me..." Chase grinned and cupped the back of Eezy's head, tugging him down into a kiss.

In answer, Eezy's mouth covered Chase's and the hungry probe of his tongue silenced any other words. Their fingers tangled in each other's hair as Duncan stood from his seat. Stripping quickly out of his uniform, he dropped it to the floor.

He lightly ran his hand along the back of Eezy's pants, along the seam. At the touch, Eezy and Chase began to undress themselves. When Eezy stood to let Chase take off his pants, Duncan reached for him, taking his own kiss. The press of his body pushed against Eezy as Chase rubbed up against Eezy's backside.

"Want to watch you two," Chase murmured, kissing a line over Eezy's shoulder.

Eezy hummed and nodded, moaning into Duncan's mouth as the navigator's hands gripped his ass, tugging him closer.

Releasing him, Duncan grinned. "On your hands and knees, Eezy."

Eezy quickly complied and Duncan reached over to the console to get out the lube. Kneeling behind Eezy, Duncan ran his hand over his cock. A moment later, he impaled Eezy, one hand gripping tightly at his hip to draw him back.

"Fuck!" Eezy rocked back, driving Duncan deeper inside. "Oh, fuck yes..."

Chase groaned and sprawled out in his seat, in perfect view to watch Duncan's cock push deep into Eezy's body. "God, you two are..." He shook his head and wrapped his fingers around his prick, pulling on it with long, slow strokes. Duncan set a quick rhythm, thrusting in and out, leaving them all breathless.

No preliminaries or foreplay was the order of the day. Intent on pleasuring both of them, the movement of Duncan's hips thrust smoothly into Eezy. Reaching up, Eezy played with his own cock while Duncan fucked him.

A low groan escaped Duncan and he looked over at Chase, watching him jerk himself off. In reaction, the push of Duncan's body became rougher and more jarring against Eezy's ass.

Chase quickened the motion of his hand, intently focused on the image in front of him, and the ragged sounds of their breathing filled the room. "Love..."

Eezy gasped. "Oh, fuck... Duncan!" Eezy shouted and jerked, cock pulsing as he came.

Duncan groaned and thrust hard, pinning Eezy tight against him as he filled the man's body. Chase followed, head falling back as he shot with a grunt.

"Oh. Damn..." Duncan slumped against Eezy.

Struggling to catch his breath, Duncan drew Eezy up and back against his chest. As Duncan rested his forehead on Eezy's shoulder, Eezy turned his head to brush a soft kiss to Duncan's hair.

"Next time you should invite me."

All three of them looked up in surprise and saw Astrasur leaning against the door frame, watching them.

Chapter Nineteen

With a faint smile, Astrasur moved toward them, his expression intense. "We should talk before we reach Brenth."

After wiping off, Chase zipped his uniform up and Eezy and Duncan put their clothes back on. None of them were the least bit self-conscious at being caught in the act. Duncan and Chase relaxed in their seats and Eezy settled himself on the arm of Duncan's chair, draping his arm around him.

"I'm not sure which was more interesting: watching the three of you play, or the conversation before you started playing," Astrasur murmured, folding his arms across his chest and making himself comfortable on the edge of the console behind him.

Duncan narrowed his gaze on the demon then glanced at the vid screen. "Seems obvious you haven't reported us for it, Astrasur. Any reason why?"

"And I won't be, I can promise you that. It's not in my best interest to report anything I've heard."

"I take it neither you nor the H-37 are exactly Interferion allies?" Chase asked quietly.

"We were until we started to hear certain things. I'm not here for a treaty, I'm here to investigate the problem and decide whether or not my world will pursue an alliance with Interferion." Astrasur shrugged, then rested his hands on the ledge of the console. "It surprised me to hear you three discussing the same problem."

"It's been bothering us lately." A tight smile creased Duncan's lips and Chase looked quickly over at him. It had been preying on them, though they hadn't really talked much about its effect.

Astrasur's gaze traveled slowly between the two of them then to Eezy, remaining silent for a long moment. "I can feel that."

When Eezy frowned, Astrasur shook his head slightly. "I'm not here to reveal any of your secrets, I'm only here to check into Interferion's dealings with Brenth."

"Oh, we have no problem revealing what we know. At least we won't once we have sufficient proof." Duncan shrugged.

"We plan on letting the cat out of the bag once all the pieces are in place, Astrasur," Chase said.

"Then I can probably be of help to you."

A slow smile crossed Duncan's lips, showing a glimpse of teeth. "And in more ways than one, I'm sure."

"You can be very sure of that." The demon's expression altered, giving a glimpse of the lust beneath the surface as his gaze traveled over the three of them. "Very sure."

Eezy and Chase chuckled, looking at each other for a moment, and Duncan slid slightly downward in his seat, his legs sprawling out in front of him. "Once we're through on Brenth, you can return with us to headquarters. We'll take the long way around."

"The three of you can escort me to meet Oera then."

"Chase will go with you, and Eezy and I will do a little scouting of our own. I don't want to waste an opportunity to do more digging at the royal palace." Duncan outlined his plan, figuring there would be a wealth of information he could get his hands on.

Eezy spoke up quietly. "You might try the royal archive rooms. They are a bit tricky to find, but it shouldn't be a problem. I can show you the way."

Duncan's brow rose, giving Eezy a look of surprise. "And how would you know that?"

Shrugging nonchalantly, Eezy replied, "I used to work there. I was a lower rank household servant."

"Then you know your way around the palace. That'll help." Duncan settled back with an air of smugness and Chase grinned at him.

* * *

After Astrasur and Chase left, Duncan and Eezy stayed on the ship, letting some time pass before they disembarked.

"Since we need to bypass the main halls, we'll have to head downstairs to the lower levels. It's doubtful we'll be noticed." Eezy appeared very confident of that, and Duncan studied him curiously as they walked down one of the smaller corridors. The few servants they passed didn't seem to notice them, so apparently Eezy was right.

"They are trained to be at the beck and call of the elite," Eezy explained. "We are not the elite."

The elaborate palace was unlike anything Duncan had ever seen. Massive white and black stones formed the walls and the ceiling arched high over their heads into a four-story structure. As they moved toward a set of stairs and went down them, the composition of the walls changed into sheets of pure crystalline Wateron. Pillars of carved Wateron lined the corridor and arched upward to form a curved V at the ceiling level. It seemed like they were walking along a hallway of ice. The light from orbs embedded in the wall reflected in glittering sparkles and danced with a fairy-like brilliance over the surface.

"King Usilusis oversaw the complete construction of this palace. He wanted a home where each planet in the Uxa galaxy was represented."

"I take it this would be Illuma," Duncan said.

Amazed, Eezy quickly glanced at Duncan. "You know quite a bit about the universe at large."

"I spent some time on Illuma. Not as much as I would have liked." Duncan had enjoyed his vacation on the planet of light and ice; he just hadn't found the time to return like he wanted to.

Leading the way through numerous turns, Eezy finally stopped in front of one of the doors and opened it. After entering, Duncan looked around at the tiny room housing one computer brain.

"All the functions of the palace are performed in this room, and all the information we need will be in here as well." Eezy grinned as he went to the small, illuminated pad screen. "We can use the Encoding Tele-Cipher Module to send the information to the ship."

As Eezy began working with the pad screen, Duncan stood beside him. On the small table, he noticed several Exodus chips and murmured, "I wonder if anybody would miss one or two of these."

Glancing down at it, Eezy shrugged. "None of them have been calibrated yet, so you could probably use them on the ship."

"That would be fucking stellward. It would certainly boost Mal's capacity." Without a second thought, Duncan pocketed two of the crysta-film protected chips.

"After we're through here, I'll have to show you the Work Station." Eezy inserted a circuit A.I., and the system began transferring to the unit. "The main component for the seeding crystals is Mucellulin. Its byproducts are made into an amazing range of products: the drug Adasanef; Lasone, an appearance enhancer; and Madalo, a highly addictive mint—to name a few."

Duncan looked over Eezy's shoulder. He placed a soft kiss to the side of Eezy's throat and whispered, "I love it when you talk dirty to me."

"I could read a Network Mechanism-Tablet manual and it would sound dirty to you."

"Umm, you're right about that." Lifting his hand, Duncan turned Eezy's head to face him. They ignored the small beeping sound from the Cipher Module, becoming momentarily lost in the hunger of their kiss.

Finally pulling back, Eezy sounded breathless. "We better go to the Work Station and then get out of here."

Reluctantly, Duncan let him go and they left the small chamber. Eezy reached for Duncan's hand, twining their fingers together. "You might find a few useful things for the ship."

Duncan didn't say anything; he simply kept a sideways glance on Eezy as they walked a few doors down then entered another room. It took a moment for Duncan to register both the enormity of the room and its contents. Slowly surveying the room, he noticed row after row of clear containers filled with liquids of every color in the spectrum. "This is a researcher's dream come true."

Moving toward one vat filled with ebony tonic, Duncan noticed the electric violet flashes flowing through the mixture. He opened the lid and the aroma of ginger filled the air. Looking quizzically over at Eezy, he asked, "Mevapa?"

When Eezy nodded, Duncan dipped his finger into the gunk and took a taste. A fruity flavor with an underlying hint of dirt burst over his taste buds. "This one doesn't taste quite ready."

"A derivative of Mucellulin and several Neulon chemicals are used to make it. It's the primary ingredient for Diusid. It needs to be processed for ten cycles. This vat is only on its seventh."

"The rarest candy in the known universe. I know. I tasted it once on CI's lips." Pausing to stare intently at the other vats, Duncan murmured, "I doubt many are aware of precisely how much Brenth contributes to Interferion coffers."

"It's all on the module, Duncan. King Usilusis allowed a certain percentage to be taken by Interferion. The rest was always sold by Brenth hands. The economy of this planet was second to none. After Oera took over, I only traveled through three of the largest cities. It is no longer what it once was. The people are not the primary concern of the royal family. Interferion money goes straight into Oera's hands and never leaves them."

Duncan helped himself to a few of the goodies as he roamed around the room.

"Not many know exactly what is going on. None but the royal family are allowed to leave the planet."

An odd look crossed Eezy's expression, but Duncan didn't know what to make of it. Going back to him, Duncan laid his hand on Eezy's shoulder. "We'll find a way to fix it, I promise. We should get back to the ship now."

Smiling wanly at him, Eezy turned away and left the room. Duncan followed behind him, aware of the dark mood clinging to Eezy. He understood it in part because if his own planet had endured what Brenth has, he would have been hot under the collar, too. While he had no desire to run his own world, its people and their way of life were still of deep interest to him.

Chapter Twenty

Chase stood silently near Astrasur, watching the diplomats surrounding and fawning over the demon. Apparently Interferion considered Astrasur and his world an alliance worth pulling all the stops out for. It had Chase wondering what Interferion wanted so badly from them. The demon lord had already spoken to Oera and his advisors, and for the moment, the two of them were mingling in the proper protocol fashion.

As the others drifted off, Astrasur glanced at Chase. "The answer to that has to do with Arrelium."

Chase shifted slightly, surprised in more ways than one by the comment. Arrelium could be used to enhance the properties of even the poorest grade of Mucellulin. The only known source of Arrelium in their dimension had long been tapped out. And the fact Astrasur had answered Chase's mental question indicated the demon could read minds.

Chase eyed the demon shrewdly. "You're a mind reader, aren't you?"

"It helps in certain situations." Amused, Astrasur stepped closer to Chase. "But with you and your navigator, it's an ability that's not really necessary."

"We do wear our lust on our sleeves," Chase murmured. "And I have no doubt Duncan and Eezy are already waiting for us to join them."

"I think we can safely leave. The counsel knows that no decision will be made until after I return to my home." When Astrasur headed for the outer door, Chase followed the quicksilver movement of his body. The smooth flex of muscle beneath skin had Chase mesmerized, and he hurriedly caught up with the demon and continued his intent study of the sleek contours of Astrasur's ass tightly encased in thin Iskya cloth.

"You could have warned us about the mind reading trick, Astrasur." As Chase quickened his step to walk beside the demon, Astrasur turned an amused smirk on him.

"It was so much more interesting not to."

Walking down the long corridor leading to the parking platform, Chase started laughing as his arm snaked around Astrasur's waist. "You're as bad as we are, my friend."

"That's saying quite a bit. Do you think Duncan and Eezy are back at the ship yet?"

"If they weren't sidetracked. You were talking to the delegation for a couple of hours." When they reached the ship, Chase opened the hatch and went inside.

The minute they entered the bridge, Duncan started in on them. "About time you two got back. You need to see this, Chase, and you, too, Astrasur."

Seeing a packaged Exodus chip laying on the console, Chase's brow rose. "Now how did that get here?"

Grinning, Duncan filled him in. "There were a few extras just lying around. The other one is already boosting Mal. Nice, huh?"

"I'll say." Laying his hand on Duncan's shoulder, Chase rubbed gently over the slippery material covering it.

"From now on, I'm just telling Arch we're requisitioning for the ship."

"I don't think that will work." Settling on the arm of Duncan's chair, Eezy pinched lightly at Duncan's side.

"Worth a try." Looking up at Chase and the demon, Duncan activated the Cipher module. "You guys are in for a treat. We've got all we need on the real treaty between Interferion and Brenth. Plus everything you ever needed to know about the processing of Mucellulin and every last damn one of its byproducts."

"I see you two were busy and not in a fun way," Astrasur murmured as he stood behind Duncan's chair, looking over at the com screen.

"It's a hell of a lot more than just seeding crystals, guys. Adasanef, Lasone, Madalo, and even Mevapa." Duncan pointed to each byproduct listed on the screen and the massive processing quantities.

"Mevapa. As in Diusid?" Chase stared at the numbers then at Duncan.

"One and the same." Duncan lost track of the conversation then when Eezy burrowed in against his throat, nuzzling him.

Chase sat down and grinned, rather content to watch. He rested a hand on his lap, pressing and kneading his hardening cock as Eezy tipped Duncan's head back for a long, deep kiss. Before Chase could get out of his seat to join them, however, a hand wrapped in his hair, tugging his head back. Staring up into the demon lord's gold eyes, Chase licked his lips just before they were captured and parted by a forked tongue.

When Eezy ended the kiss, Duncan became entranced by the sight of his husband and the demon. A low groan escaped him as Eezy delivered hard bites to the side of his throat. A hand strayed to the front of Duncan's pants, kneading over the growing bulge. Without a word, Eezy wiggled out of his uniform and stood, drawing Duncan with him.

"Come on," Eezy murmured, moving around behind Duncan. "Want to taste..." He undressed Duncan slowly, just as Astrasur undressed Chase.

"I want inside you," Astrasur murmured to Chase.

Chase shivered as the demon's voice rumbled near his ear. "Yes. Fuck, yes." He caught Duncan's gaze and smiled, mouthing 'I love you' just as his uniform hit the floor. Astrasur's large hand wrapped around his cock, short-circuiting Chase's brain and making him moan. "Oh, fuck..."

Grinning, Duncan knew they were both in for it. As he was undressed, his eyes never wavered from Chase. "Always, babe."

Eezy knelt behind him, hands massaging over the firm globes of Duncan's ass. When Duncan shifted, spreading his legs apart, Eezy leaned in, thumbs opening Duncan. The feel of Eezy's tongue probing inside him made Duncan's breath catch in his throat.

Chase groaned at the sight, shuddering slightly when Astrasur stroked him slowly. The demon backed up, then sat down, pulling his own cock out from the folds of his clothing. Chase got a quick glimpse, eyes widening when he saw the length.

"Oh, damn..." Chase fumbled in the com drawer for the lube and popped the cap. After pouring a good amount on the head of Astrasur's cock, he slicked his hand down the long, thick shaft. "Fuck, you're huge."

Astrasur chuckled and grabbed Chase's hips, turning him to face Duncan. "Just imagine, Captain Sykes," he said, pulling Chase down to straddle his thighs, "how it will feel inside you." As the demon's cock pierced his body, Chase shook, head falling back as he moaned and hissed.

Eezy bent Duncan over even more, driving his tongue deeper, licking and sucking at the puckered skin. His own cock was leaking steadily as he pushed two fingers deep inside Duncan. "Need you," he whispered, biting lightly at Duncan's right ass cheek as he finger-fucked him.

Rapt in the sight before him and the sensation arousing his body, Duncan grew weak in the knees. His body tightened as he leaned back, burying Eezy's fingers deeper in his ass. When the fingers withdrew, Duncan went to his knees and one arm snaked around him as the head of Eezy's cock slid between his ass cheeks..

Grabbing the lube from the arm of the chair, Eezy slicked his own cock. A moment later the hard pressure filled Duncan and left them both panting. The movement of Chase's body, grinding over the demon's cock, and the feel of Eezy's prick deep inside him, scattered Duncan's wits.

"Astrasur," Chase moaned the demon's name, hips jerking as one of Astrasur's hands closed around his cock again.

"Holy shit," Eezy panted as he leaned over Duncan's back. "So fucking hot. You both are."

One hand entangling in Eezy's hair, Duncan turned his head and silenced Eezy with a hard kiss. Pure need rushed through Duncan and he shuddered as Eezy's hand stroked quickly over his cock.

Astrasur's teeth closed over Chase's throat and his fingers danced in their own pattern over the thick flesh, igniting a sharper need. All four of them were caught in the sensual erotic rhythm, their bodies joined and the room filled with the deep sounds and cries of that pleasure.

Breaking away from the kiss, Duncan gasped out, "Harder, Eezy. Harder. Close."

Chase cried out, fingers digging into the arms of the seat as he rode the demon lord's quick thrusts. "Don't stop! Oh, fuck, don't stop..."

Eezy groaned and gripped Duncan's hip with his free hand, jerking him back hard onto his cock. Matching the demon's thrusts into Chase, Eezy picked up the near-brutal rhythm, slamming over and over into Duncan's ass.

Unable to stop the waves of sensation, Duncan came suddenly, his release spurting over Eezy's hand and onto the floor. His sharp cry echoed in the cabin and he reached back to grip tightly to Eezy's hip. Eezy's cock pulsed inside Duncan as he came, the strain of his body molding to Duncan's back.

Chase followed behind them, body going taut seconds before he shouted, his come pouring over the demon's fist. Astrasur gave another hard thrust and roared, head falling back as he filled Chase. Speechless, Chase slumped in Astrasur's arms, breathless and shaking.

* * *

After dropping the demon lord off at Interferion headquarters, neither Duncan nor Chase waited around for their next set of orders. If Arch wanted them for something, he'd contact them later. As soon as they boarded the ship, Chase put Mal on automatic and they all retreated to their cabin. Duncan seriously wanted and needed some alone time with the two men he loved more than life. He knew Chase had been feeling the same.

When the cabin door shut behind them, Duncan stripped out of his uniform and tossed it to the side. Climbing into the huge bed, he watched silently as Chase and Eezy began to undress as well.

Chase held out a hand to Eezy. "You belong here," he said, taking Eezy's hand. He pulled Eezy close and kissed him softly. "With us."

Rolling over to his side, Duncan's hand caressed lightly over Eezy's bare ass. "He's right. You're a part of us now."

Though nothing had ever been said, it had become very clear that Duncan's emotions were tangled both with Chase and Eezy. Not something he planned on, but something he had no intention of letting go of.

"I never intended any of this," Eezy said, looking from Chase to Duncan. "But I can't imagine being without either of you."

"Shh..." Chase smiled and pressed a finger to Eezy's lips. "You won't have to be without us."

Duncan reached for both of them, drawing them down to the bed. "I'm hoping by now you understand just how much we both want you to stay with us."

For a brief moment, uncertainty flickered in Eezy's eyes, but he didn't say anything.

Duncan looked over at Chase, nodding slightly with a smile. "Maybe we should just tell him, love."

Propping himself up on his arm, Chase leaned over Eezy, who was sandwiched between them. "I love you," he whispered on Eezy's lips. "We both do, Eezy."

"Others come and go in our lives, Eezy. We have fun with them and I've never regretted a minute of it. We've been the only two who have stayed. Now we want you to stay as well. He's right, we both love you." Duncan's fingers grazed slowly over Eezy's arm, then he drew Chase's hand to rest with his on Eezy's chest.

Eezy still didn't say anything, but a great deal reflected in his eyes. Drawing a deep breath, he finally said, "You two are the only ones who have ever wanted me to stay around. I believe I'll love you long past the time either of you want me."

"Then we have the rest of our lives to experience it." Chase smiled and kissed Eezy, then pulled Duncan down to join them, turning it into a three-way kiss. One of Eezy's hands joined theirs, all three of them holding on.

* * *

Several hours later, after Duncan and Chase went back to the bridge, Eezy sat on the bed, leaning against the headboard. He was anything but relaxed. Staring vacantly at the picture of the captain and the navigator hanging on the wall, Eezy felt lost. How could he explain everything he needed to?

A voice came over the communicator embedded in his head, and he closed his eyes, focusing on the message.

"You've been quiet lately," the soft-spoken voice said.

"I've already sent a report, V. Everything is as it's supposed to be." What else could he say? For the time being everything was what he wanted, but how long would that last once Duncan and Chase knew the truth?

"I saw it. How are you, really?"

"Everything will be fine. How do you think I feel?" The dull monotone of Eezy's internal voice revealed a great more than he wanted it to. Scooting lower onto the bed, he rolled onto his stomach and buried his face against his arm.

V sighed softly. *"They're good men,"* he said, *"but so are you. I think they will understand."*

"I'm not so sure of that, V. I've lied to them. After tonight, I don't know how they will take it." Eezy was deeply troubled. Though he had no choice but to do as he did, he hadn't counted on any real emotion developing between any of them. Now that it had, it left him in more pain than he could have imagined when all of this started.

V remained silent for a long moment. *"This has gone deeper than anyone intended, hasn't it?"*

"Far beyond what was intended. At the start, they were a means to an end for me. How could I ever explain that away?" Somehow Eezy doubted anybody would be able to get past that once everything was known. He realized how every one of his actions would be seen, no matter how his own feelings had changed.

"You love them," V said simply. *"I've known you for quite some time, my friend. A matter of the heart is something you can't hide from me. Do they know?"*

"They both told me tonight how much they love me, and I told them the same. I shouldn't have. It wasn't supposed to turn out this way." In the beginning, he'd had control over everything and now he was in over his head.

"Sometimes... the answers to our prayers are not what we intended."

"I will be returning home shortly, V." Cutting off the communication between them, Eezy tried to burrow deeper into the bed. Somehow, he doubted he would still have a place with Duncan and Chase when it all ended.

Episode Six: Life in the Fast Lane

Chapter Twenty-One

"Release the anthropomorphic, psychopathic android monkeys and the terrifyingly horrendous kekabibble!" Rudolpho screamed the command to Nerk as he frantically jumped out of the way of the portal.

"Whoa, Rudy, not this time." Duncan tried to head off the siege of monkeys but was too late. The metallic chimps poured through the portal, searching for their target. Right behind them, the kekabibble hopped out of the gateway and stomped several of the monkeys in its path. Pulling Eezy out of the way, Duncan made it to safe ground on the Tribpolya platform.

Because they didn't have time to wait for Rudolpho's plan to fail, Chase moved quickly toward Nerk. "Get them back in the portal. We've got to talk to Rudy."

Momentarily confused, Nerk stared at him before he began to recalibrate the portal.

"Nerk, you nitwit fool! What are you doing?" I command you to let the monkeys go." An irate Rudolpho advanced on the Riseon, but Duncan headed him off. Grabbing Rudolpho's arm, Duncan pulled him away from the portal generator.

"We're not here to steal, Rudy. We need your help with something." Chase jumped down from the platform to help Nerk shut down the generator, then turned to address Rudolpho again. "We'll make it worth your time."

Eezy remained on the platform, letting the other two handle the situation.

"My help? My help! You two are out of your minds! Nerk! How dare you disobey my order, you poor excuse for a feebleminded assistant!"

To calm him down, Duncan pulled the Fission Atomo Pack from underneath his jacket and waved the small black box in the air. "Interested in this? It's worth fifty thousand creds."

The second Rudolpho saw the box, he calmed slightly and eyed Duncan with a calculating look. A hint of suspicion laced his tone when he finally spoke. "What are you two up to now?"

"We just want you to advertise some information for us, Rudy. That's all. And that little beauty will be yours," Chase explained.

"Advertise what? Why?" Rudolpho rapidly fired the questions at them, never once looking away from the pack in Duncan's hand.

Handing Rudolpho the compu-pad, Chase waited for him to read over it. Duncan laid the Atomo on top of the nearby table and answered his questions. "We just want you to open every one of your channels both under and above ground and our message out. You've got access and a network to every damn planet in the known universe."

Shock crossed Rudolpho's features as he scanned the text on the screen. "You want me to send this out? You've got to be kidding me. It's a joke, right?"

"There you're wrong, Rudy. Our bosses are on the bad side, and we're going to make it right," Duncan casually commented.

"You're working for CI?" Curious now, Rudolpho shut the pad then looked at both of them.

"Yes and no. We're working to clear up the misinformation about him, but he doesn't know us," Chase answered.

"Only you two would be idiotic enough to do something like this." Rudolpho barked out a short laugh. "I'll do it. If you want it out to everybody, it'll take me a while, but it will get out. I suggest you two find a way to vacate this universe before Interferion finds out."

"We've got our own agenda, Rudy." Grinning, Duncan draped his arm around Eezy and eased him closer.

"It's been nice knowing you, Rudy. You take care." Chase held out his hand to shake Rudolpho's.

Taking the hand, a wry smile creased Rudolpho's lips. "I really can't believe you two are doing this. Good luck."

Nerk stared at them, astounded, and Duncan quipped, "Rudy, you need to pay Nerk. I mean really."

Confused, Rudolpho shook his head. "Why would I pay my own son?"

Startled into laughter, Eezy murmured, "Guess that explains that."

* * *

Duncan sprawled in his chair, laughing uproariously. Trying to catch his breath, he managed to gasp out, "Did you see his face?"

"I don't think Rudy expected the change of plans from our side." Chase grabbed a hold of Eezy, drawing him back against his chest. His other hand slid along the line of Eezy's hip.

"It probably won't take him all that long to get the message out, so I think we should get our asses out of here." Eezy tried to maintain a certain amount of level-headedness, but he was quickly losing the battle with the errant caresses from Chase's hand.

"Oh, I think Chase has a better idea. We'll let Mal do the work while we play." Duncan stood and stepped closer to Eezy, divesting Eezy of his clothing.

"Mal, take us into orbit around Quadrant L, Sector BR-11." Once he'd given the order, Chase turned his attention back to Eezy and Duncan. The press of his lips brushing to Eezy's ear, he whispered, "We'll have plenty of time to enjoy you, Eezy."

When Chase's teeth bit lightly at his ear lobe, Eezy shivered. "Both of you can turn me from worried to wanting to be fucked in no time flat."

Duncan's hands roamed the bare skin of Eezy's chest as he leaned in for a kiss. The pinch of his fingers to Eezy's nipples punctuated his words. "A talent we like to share."

Unable to resist touching, Eezy pulled open the front of Duncan's uniform and his fingers began their own exploration. Duncan's tongue pushed between Eezy's lips, silencing the soft sound of his moan. Chase's tongue and teeth tasted the line of flesh bared by the tilt of Eezy's head.

Before long, all three of them were naked and pressed to each other. The grind of their bodies igniting a sharper fire between them. After several long moments, the sound of their breathing had become distinctly labored.

"Against the wall, Eezy." Duncan stepped away from him, searching for the lube. Eezy moved to the one bare space on the wall and placed his hands flat against it. Spreading his legs, he pushed his ass out in a tantalizing invitation.

Chase stared hungrily at him, one hand lowering to stroke over his own cock. "Fuck, I have to have that."

Duncan smiled as he opened the tube of gel. "Oh, you will, babe. And I'm going to have you." Moving in front of him, Duncan squirted some of the gel on Chase's cock then watched the captain's hand spread it over the hard flesh.

Watching them intently, Eezy's breath quickened and the restless shift of his body begged for attention. After Duncan took care of his own cock, he dropped the lube then gently pushed Chase toward Eezy.

Chase went to Eezy, his hands going for that sweet ass, fingers massaging the flesh. The head of his cock probed between Eezy's cheeks, drawing a moan from both of them. Duncan was right behind him and the insistent pressure of his prick filled Chase as he lowered his head and bit at Chase's shoulder.

It began in a slow, easy rhythm, punctuated by their sighs. Touching and caressing each other, their hands never remained still nor did their bodies. Eezy found himself pinned against the wall and each of Duncan's thrusts into Chase drove Chase deeper into Eezy.

One hand clawed at the wall and Eezy groaned. "You both are incredible. It feels so fucking perfect."

Chase whispered in Eezy's ear, "It is. You are."

The soft tone of Duncan's voice followed Chase's. "You belong to both of us now."

There was nothing inside Eezy that could argue that. Tipping his head back, he closed his eyes and his breath escaped him in another moan when Chase began to fuck him in earnest. His hips pushed back to each filling motion and

Eezy's hand dropped to his painfully hard cock. Rubbing his thumb over the head, the slick liquid smeared over his skin before he started stroking over himself, imitating the hard thrusts into him.

The earlier gentleness had faded, driven by the deeper need riding all three of them. No more words were left, only the primal sounds of mutual passion. Duncan's fingers gripped tightly to Chase's hips and, in turn, Chase's nails clawed into Eezy. Quickening the pace of his hand, a hard spasm rocked through Eezy before he came, shooting over his hand and hitting the wall.

A sharp grunt followed from Chase before the hard line of his body strained into Eezy in the shuddering throes of release. The jarring motion of Duncan's body against them continued for a moment longer before his cry of pleasure filled their senses.

Eezy clung to the wall, his legs threatening to give way under him. When both men drew back, Chase quickly picked up Eezy and carried him through the ship to their cabin. Duncan followed behind them and after Chase put Eezy down on the bed, they both crawled in with him, one on each side.

"My life has never been like this." Eezy was still lost in the afterglow of the passion he'd feasted on.

Raising on his elbow, Duncan dropped a soft kiss to Eezy's lips. "It'll be this way for as long as you allow it."

Eezy's gaze traveled between the two, seeing the open expressions of emotions on both of their faces. "You two love so unconditionally. I've never met anyone like you." He didn't think he would ever meet their like again, either.

"Welcome to life in the fast lane, Eezy." Duncan laughed as his fingers rubbed teasingly over Eezy's chest.

"We're all in this together. What's our next move going to be?" Chase held Duncan's gaze with a questioning look.

"We really should make a stop at headquarters. I don't want to leave Arch clueless when it all comes out."

Chase nodded his approval. "Yeah, I agree, love. It's going to be like a room full of Nuclear-powered Explosive Biochips, all going off at once. No reason to leave poor Arch uninformed."

"It's going to be more like a planet full."

"Yeah, the fireworks will be interesting," Eezy muttered.

"We're not going to allow anything to harm you." Chase's finger trailed over Eezy's lower lip.

"Eezy, you already know we would do anything for you," Duncan said. "You can be damn sure we still will."

With a determined effort, Eezy smiled and relaxed. "I know. Given your reputations, everything will be fine. I just worry a little."

"Mal, headquarters." Chase gave the order and Mal answered cheerfully: "On course, Captain."

Rolling onto his back, Duncan folded his arms behind his head and Eezy curled up to his side. Chase molded against Eezy's back, one hand lightly caressing up and down Eezy's hip. Chase's grin widened with a wicked edge.

"In the meantime, I think we can amuse ourselves in far more interesting ways than just laying here talking."

Chapter Twenty-Two

Brushing past Arch's clerk, Duncan and Chase barged into their boss' office, Eezy following quietly behind them.

"I was wondering when you guys would show up." Arch regarded them calmly as he stood and went to one of his cabinets.

Eezy remained behind the captain and navigator, folding his hands behind his back as the other two marched right up to Arch's desk.

"I really don't believe you're involved in this, Arch. But President Xere is in up to his eyeballs. He's been using Interferion as his own personal playground for power." Duncan leaned against the desk, reciting the facts quietly.

"We just wanted to give you the heads up before the shit hits the universal fan." Chase dropped the papers in his hand in front of his boss. "And it will, as soon as Rudy broadcasts it."

"I know, boys. I've known all along. Why do you think you've been getting the missions you have been? Every last one of them was designed to give you a clue to the puzzle. I knew I could rely on you two to put it all together and do the right thing." With a smug air, Arch studied them.

"You knew?" Confused, Duncan blinked and shook his head.

"I've known CI for a very long time. I knew he wasn't guilty of the crimes Interferion accused him of, but I had no proof." When Arch glanced over at Eezy, Eezy refused to meet his gaze.

Neither Duncan or Chase said anything, watching the other two. Finally Eezy raised his eyes to Arch's and said, "I thought you were in on it, Arch."

"No, I had to bide my time. I couldn't afford to lose my position if I wanted to find the truth of what was going on." Arch reached into his desk and drew out a small silver orb. "You two will need this for the time being. I'll do my best to minimize the fall out damage that could hit you guys. But everything still isn't fully under control here, and once the news gets out, you both will be hunted."

"You've giving us control of a class M upgrader?" Chase took the orb, eyeing Arch questioningly.

After nodding to Chase, Arch addressed Eezy. "Several of the old Pretoria are already here and waiting for you. When the chaos reaches Brenth, you'll need to be at the helm."

Confused, Chase glanced back at Eezy and saw the commanding figure of CI instead. Seeing Chase's expression, Duncan whirled around and stared at CI in shock. Neither he nor Chase could quite believe what they were seeing.

With a slight nod, CI spoke quietly. "I know. Oera will run and leave the Order to collapse in on itself." Taking a step toward Duncan and Chase, CI faltered then stopped. "I apologize to both of you. When my brother told me what you did for him, I decided to find out more about you myself."

A pained expression crossed Duncan's face as he stared wordlessly at CI. In the next second, Chase moved closer to the navigator, his arm encircling Duncan almost protectively. Chase's voice rose slightly, anger rising through the shock.

"You used us?"

"No. That's not… I never meant to…" Gesturing helplessly, CI couldn't say another word. An air of desolation clung to him, seeming to age him in the space of a moment. With a clearly determined effort, a blandly neutral look fixed upon his face. "I will return to Brenth." Without another word, he spun on his heel and left Arch's office. Duncan simply stared unblinkingly at the empty space.

"You two better get out of here before those broadcasts go out," Arch said, breaking the awkward, almost painful silence.

Chase turned to face him. "Where the hell will we go? They know where to find Duncan's family home."

"You might find more safety than you think in orbit around Oshshar."

Chase glared at him with the mention of one of Brenth's moons. "Are you mad? Have you no idea what has happened? Have you no idea that we took a man into our lives, our hearts, only to find that it was all a lie?" Tightening his arm around Duncan, Chase dragged his navigator out of Arch's office, leaving Arch staring helplessly as they walked out the door.

* * *

Chase watched Duncan silently as the navigator set their course. A dark, brooding mood had settled over Duncan, and they had yet to talk about it.

When they returned to the ship, Duncan had thrown himself into more work than the two of them had ever done in their entire careers. As Duncan turned away from the console, Chase held out his hand to him. At first it looked like Duncan would ignore it. Hurt, Chase lowered his hand.

Seeing the pained expression, Duncan quickly stepped forward and took Chase's hand. "I'm sorry, love."

With a tug, Chase pulled Duncan to him and onto his lap. "It won't help if you keep it all inside."

Stricken by remorse, Duncan tried to speak but ended up sliding his arms around Chase and burying his face in the captain's hair.

Drawing a deep, steadying breath, Chase held him. They had both received one hell of an unexpected shock. When it had faded, Chase had been able to think more clearly, but he wasn't sure his husband was in the same state. Chase really didn't blame Eezy for the deception. CI's position had been such that he couldn't have known Chase and Duncan were trying to help him. By the time the obvious would have become apparent, it would have been too late because CI was already living the lie of being Eezy.

"I understand, but I don't." Duncan's whisper still carried a hint of the emotional pain Chase knew the navigator tried desperately to hide.

His hand smoothed over Duncan's hair in a comforting touch. "I don't think he had a choice, love."

"He could have told us after we went to Rudy."

"True, but I have the feeling he was afraid we would reject him." Chase could think quite a bit more clearly now that the shock had worn off.

"But how much of it was a lie?"

Duncan asked the burning question and Chase's arm tightened around him. He had to answer him honestly. "I don't know, Duncan. You are usually far more intuitive than I am."

In the long silence that followed, Duncan clung all the more tightly to Chase. Both of Chase's hands slide up into Duncan's hair and drew his head forward. He could see Duncan was hurt beyond his own ability to express it.

Without a word, Chase tried to calm the internal struggle so apparent in Duncan's face. The touch of his lips gently coaxed Duncan to open to him, and a moment later the navigator finally responded, his lips parting to the soft enticement of Chase's tongue.

Chase wanted to soothe and take away the pain for him. He could feel Duncan's desperate need in the tighter press of his body. Chase would broach the subject of going to Brenth later, but for now, both of them needed the time just to themselves. Something Chase gladly gave to Duncan. Slowly, he began to undress Duncan, his fingers sliding the uniform from his shoulders. The caressing touch over his back drew a small shiver from Duncan. The navigator squirmed his way out of the jacket, letting it drop to the floor. Duncan only broke away to get rid of his shoes and pants then quickly returned to Chase's lap.

This time was solely for his husband. Each touch of Chase's hands and lips conveyed the love Chase held. Clinging to him, Duncan arched slightly as Chase's hand drifted lower.

"I love you," Chase whispered as he curled his fingers around Duncan's length. He gave it a slow stroke, from base to tip.

The heat of Duncan's breath warmed Chase's skin as the navigator sighed quietly. Duncan made no real attempt to touch Chase other than an aimless drifting of his fingers back and forth against Chase's shoulder.

With his other hand, Chase cupped the back of Duncan's neck and held him close, licking and sucking the smooth, sensitive skin just at the side of his neck. He worked Duncan's cock slowly, never stopping but never speeding up. While the desire was strong, he was unhurried, letting Duncan take what he needed at his own pace.

A slight jerk of Duncan's hips encouraged the movement of Chase's hand. When Chase turned his head slightly, Duncan's teeth nipped gently on the lobe of his ear then nuzzled lower to his throat. A soft groan began then quickly rose, followed by a more demanding nudge of Duncan's hips.

Chase's head fell back, giving Duncan more room. The strokes picked up in speed, Chase's fingers tight with every pull. "Duncan..." He rocked his hips up, pushing his still-covered erection against Duncan, searching for friction.

"Need you so much." One of Duncan's hands slid down, fingers opening the front of Chase's pants and wrapping tightly around Chase's cock. It wouldn't take much to send both of them over the edge and with a harsh grunt, Duncan's came in Chase's hand. As he buried his face against Chase's throat, his body shuddered repeatedly.

"Duncan!" Chase thrust into Duncan's fist, groaning as he came. "Oh, God..." He kissed Duncan's head, eyes closing tightly, aftershocks still rippling through him.

The soft touch of Duncan's lips trailed over Chase's skin as they both clung to each other. When Duncan's breath finally returned to normal, he lifted his head, resting it against Chase's. "I love you so much, babe."

Chase didn't open his eyes, barely even took a breath. "I..." He shook his head, swallowed hard. God, he felt like he was unraveling at the seams. All he could do was tighten his hold on Duncan.

Immediately Duncan sensed the struggle inside Chase. He opened his eyes and drew his head back, sliding his arms around Chase's neck. "What, love?"

When he opened his eyes, Chase looked up into Duncan's. "I love you," he said quietly, "but I can't let him go anymore than I can let you go."

The look in Duncan's eyes dulled and he ended up dropping his gaze to Chase's shirt. "I'm not sure if it's an option, Chase."

Slipping a finger beneath Duncan's chin, Chase tilted his head back up. "Can you honestly say you don't love him enough to try?"

"He'd come to us." Duncan finally met his gaze squarely. From his set expression, it appeared Duncan was highly doubtful of any real interest on CI's part.

"Put yourself in his place, love. Would you?"

"In his place, no, I wouldn't, but then he wouldn't have any real reason to. He rules Brenth now. He got what he wanted." Not really wanting to discuss it, Duncan climbed off Chase's lap and gathered up his uniform.

Chase sighed and let him go. After watching Duncan for a moment, he tucked himself back into his pants, wiping his hand on the towel he'd used in the engine room before they set out. He didn't know how to change Duncan's mind, but he figured there had to be something he could do. He sure as hell wasn't going to give up either of his men that easily.

* * *

Duncan worked in the back bay, trying for the umpteen millionth time to get the Tactical Probe-Deflector operational. With a frustrated sigh, he eyed the wrench next to his hand. No matter what he did, the damn orb would not spin properly in its metal housing. They would have to install the new one. Something Duncan did not look forward to.

Carefully, he began dismantling the old TCD. If the connections weren't unlinked in the proper order, the damn thing could melt the entire casing. That would mean technicians would have to work on it, which meant at least a day docked in repair. Since he and Chase were basically on the run, that wasn't an option.

Once Duncan had the couplers safely unlinked, he slowly pulled out the old orb. He tried to keep his thoughts from wandering while he worked. After dumping the orb into its old container, he unpacked the new one. Even though the work was painstaking and mind numbing, he had no real luck in keeping his thoughts from drifting toward Eezy. Or CI, he thought with a bitter edge.

God, it hurt to realize the whole time Eezy had only been trying to get information from them. Eezy could have said something after he realized Duncan and Chase were on his side. But he hadn't. Growling softly to himself, Duncan twisted one of the couplers a little too tightly. Thankfully it didn't break and he resumed connecting the orb in the hollowed-out metal circle.

He knew damn well it wasn't likely Chase would let go of the idea of going after CI. But how to shield his husband from the fallout of further rejection was beyond Duncan. They both were already deeply hurt enough. Duncan wasn't sure he could handle anymore. But he'd always be there for Chase.

The urge to just smash the orb rose in Duncan, along with an overwhelming anger. Carefully laying aside the wrench in his hand, Duncan took several deep breaths to calm himself.

Convincing Chase that going after CI was a bad idea would probably not be easy. None of this would be. He wanted Eezy back as much as Chase did. Too many memories continued to play in his head, and Duncan couldn't shut them out. Maybe he needed to convince himself of just how stupid it would be to go after Eezy before he could convince Chase of the same.

Chapter Twenty-Three

CI sat on his throne, watching the parade of men and women before him. Oera's harem now belonged to him, but he really see the gleaming, oil-slicked limbs and bodies trying so enticingly to get his attention. He hurt too much inside to take notice of anything but important planetary decisions.

One young man knelt and began washing Cyril's feet. Cyril felt the light touch, but it really didn't affect him. Vilichr entered and the sharp clap of his hands instantly dismissed the harem. Everyone silently hurried toward the outer chamber, not daring to disobey the order. When the doors shut, Vilichr walked up to the throne. Cyril felt the weight of his friend's knowing gaze.

"I have delivered the revised treaty to Arch. It should give him something to negotiate with and keep him, Duncan, and Chase out of serious trouble."

"I appreciate that, V. I don't want any of them punished for aiding me."

A wry smile twisted the ambassador's lips. "Given the choice of a complete shut down of trade or a return of the old treaty, I think Interferion will be grateful you aren't shutting them off completely. It will give Arch the leverage he needs to stay on the Interferion payroll."

"But what about Duncan and Chase? Are they safe?" Cyril tried but couldn't stop the desperate need to know from showing.

"They were chased by a class H star cruiser, but they outran it. They're in orbit around Qiw-Te. I can send a class R to intercept them and bring them here if you want."

"No," he vetoed the idea immediately. "Neither of them would appreciate being forced here." No matter how much he wanted the two safely with him, he wouldn't force them.

"Since it isn't likely that Interferion will send a battle cruiser after them, they'll be fine where they are." Moving close enough to lean down over him, Vilichr laid his hand on Cyril's, giving him a shrewd look. "You want both of them here, but until Brenth is fully secure, you can't chase after them. So let me."

Closing his eyes, Cyril wanted to believe that everything could be made right between Duncan, Chase, and himself. Despair enveloped his heart, and he felt he would never be whole again. Too many memories reminded him of how it had been between the three of them. Part of Cyril knew he would give up his kingdom if only Chase and Duncan would take him back.

Reacting to the open show of pain on CI's face, Vilichr dropped to his knees in front of him and gathered Cyril's hands in his. "My old friend, you love both of them deeply. Allow me to go talk to them."

Torn between the hope of having them back and the pain of the image of when he had last seen them, Cyril couldn't speak. Drawing a deep breath, he opened his eyes and saw his own haunted visage in the reflection of Vilichr's eyes. "When they found out, they were so hurt. I can't forget. I never meant—"

The ambassador didn't let him finish. "I know, Cyril. I know you too well." One hand lightly touched the king's cheek, and Vilichr was clearly determined as he added, "I am going to talk to them."

* * *

When Vilichr's face flashed on the com screen, Chase stared at it blankly for a moment, wondering why the hell the ambassador was signaling him. Leaning forward, he opened the communication channel.

"Chase, I'm asking for permission to board the ship."

"Of course." Chase punched in the security code and sat back, still staring at the com as it went to black again.

Several long moments later, the sound of the connector arms clanged into place as the ship docked with Chase's. Chase checked the view screen to see Duncan still fast asleep in their cabin. Chase was able to relax, knowing Duncan would remain asleep. He really wasn't so sure how the navigator would react. Leaning back in his chair, he glanced up when Vilichr entered the bridge.

Without giving Chase a chance to say anything, the ambassador spoke. "I'm here to talk about CI, Chase."

Chase sighed and waved a hand toward the navigator's chair. "Please, have a seat."

After sitting down in the seat, Vilichr regarded Chase with a level look. Never one to beat around the bush, he quickly stated his purpose for being there. "I want both of you to go with me to Brenth. Just hear him out."

Lifting an eyebrow, Chase glanced back toward the door leading out of the bridge. "I'm not sure Duncan will go for that, Ambassador." He looked back at Vilichr. "But I'm willing to."

"I can't even begin to explain how Cyril feels, Chase." Vilichr slid out of his chair, went to Chase, dropped to his knees in front of the captain. "But I can tell you I don't like you calling me ambassador in that formal tone."

Chase looked down at him, then smiled slightly. "I'm sorry, Vilichr. It's just been..." He sighed and shook his head. "We opened our lives... our hearts... to him, only to find that he'd been using us." He lifted a hand when Vilichr opened his mouth to respond. "But... I understand why he did it. I want him back, Vilichr. I want both of my men in my arms... but I'm not so sure Duncan is going to be so easily convinced of anything."

Remaining silent to let Chase finish, Vilichr rested his hand over Chase's, giving it a gentle squeeze. "I understand it's been very rough. But I think all of you need the chance to talk to each other. So many things aren't what they seem."

"That's the understatement of the century," Chase replied dryly. "All right. I'll go. I doubt Duncan will, though."

Rising to his feet, Vilichr drew Chase up to stand as well. "Then we'll leave him out of the equation for the moment. Hopefully we'll be able to convince him later."

"How deep were you in this?"

Sighing quietly, Vilichr kept hold of Chase's hand, leading him out of the bridge and toward the back bay. "I knew what Interferion was trying to do to him, but I had no proof. I also knew how deeply entangled Cyril was becoming with both of you."

They boarded Vilichr's ship and as soon as the door closed and sealed, Chase turned to him. "How did you know so much?"

"I've known him all my life. And before you ask, no, we aren't lovers," Vilichr quickly reassured him. Settling at the helm, the ambassador punched in the return coordinates. "Cyril is on Brenth, waiting for us."

Chase sat down next to him. "Well, that's a relief. No offense."

"You might be surprised to know that while Cyril now has Oera's harem at his beck and call, he hasn't touched any of them." He filled Chase in on a few of the things happening. By the time they reached the docking bay at Brenth, the captain had lapsed into a thoughtful silence. Pushing the switch for the entry door, Vilichr turned in his seat to face Chase.

When the seal hissed into place, Chase took a deep breath and stood. "Let's do this before I lose my nerve."

They walked silently into the bay, then Vilichr led him down the halls to the throne room. When they reached the throne room, Vilichr opened the door and stepped aside to let Chase enter.

"The next shipment will not be sent until I receive word on the acceptance of the new treaty. The quota allotted is near completed, so I suggest you revise the invoices to reflect the new changes." A stern eye held to his advisor's as Cyril continued, "If you plan on keeping your position, I suggest you don't gainsay me."

When Chase entered the room, Cyril fell completely silent before he motioned the advisor to leave the room. The advisor bowed and backed away from the dais, then turned and left the room. When the door closed, Chase realized that he and CI were alone. He opened his mouth to speak, but no words came out. Though the appearance was far different from that of Eezy, the ruler's eyes remained the same, and Chase found himself walking toward the dais without fully realizing it.

Shock held Cyril in place as Chase advanced on him. Hungrily, he drank in the familiar sight of the captain and he couldn't remain still for long. Before Chase made it halfway across the throne room, Cyril was on his feet, moving toward him.

As they came to stand before each other, Chase took a deep breath and looked into Cyril's eyes. Finding the words was so hard...

"Looks like you're doing well," he said quietly.

"I didn't think you would come here. I thought I would never see you again." Cyril had to bite back the rest of the words before his pain became any more evident.

Stepping closer, Chase reached up, cupping Cyril's cheek with his palm. "You think we are so willing to let you go?"

Closing his eyes, CI drew a shuddering breath as his face rubbed against the touch of Chase's hand. "Would you even believe me if I told you how much I love you?"

"Cyril." Chase leaned in, lips close to Cyril's. "You don't have to tell me. I already know." Without giving Cyril a chance to respond, Chase caught him in a soft kiss, pouring everything he couldn't find the words for into it.

Pure need assaulted Cyril and his lips parted in a pained sound, letting Chase take over. Stepping closer, his arms encircled Chase's neck and his body molded to the captain's.

A hungry desperation overwhelmed both of them as Cyril opened to him.

Hands falling to Cyril's waist, Chase held him close, the kiss turning hard, desperate. Only the need for breath stopped the kiss and Chase pinned Cyril with a heated gaze. "Show me," he said breathlessly as he began backing Cyril toward the throne. "Show me I haven't lost you."

Cyril would have given him anything and everything he asked for. The robe he wore was quickly stripped off and left on the floor. Unable to remain silent, he gave voice to his own thoughts. "What do you want, Chase? I give you anything and everything."

"You. With us." Chase advanced on him, fingers working quickly to rid the captain of his own clothes. "Where you belong, Cyril." Once he was nude, he reached out and tugged Cyril against him, flesh against heated flesh. "No more bullshit. No more running. We love you too much to let you go without a fight."

"You have it." It required no thought on his part because Chase and Duncan were what he wanted. Cyril knew that now. The slow rub of his body ran along the captain's, inciting both of them, his hands starting at Chase's chest then trailed slowly downward toward his nipples. Lowering his head, Cyril drew one into his mouth and bit, his fingers pinching sharply at the other.

Chase hissed, fingers going to Cyril's hair, fists tightening. "Cyril... yes..." He groaned and tugged Cyril's head up, pushing his tongue into the ruler's mouth as he wrapped the fingers of one hand around Cyril's length. He stopped the kiss long enough to breathe "love you" across Cyril's lips, then dove back in as his thumb grazed the tip of his lover's cock.

The sound of need was swallowed by Chase's mouth; the arch of Cyril's body pressed closer. They remained locked in the embrace until Cyril drew his head back and went down to his knees. One of his hands caressed upward over Chase's thigh as the other wrapped around the base of Chase's cock, guiding it into his mouth.

Shuddering, Chase rested his hands on Cyril's head, not guiding, just touching. It seemed like ages since he'd felt this touch, those lips. He tried to speak, wanting to rain praise and love down on Cyril, but all that came out was a low moan when his lover's throat encased his cock in slick heat.

Wanting Chase lost in all the pleasure he could give him, Cyril took the entire length deeply into his mouth, lips tightening to suck the hard flesh. Looking upward, his expression reflected his own fascination with the sight and feel of his lover. Literally at that moment, Cyril worshipped him and was showing it. Beginning slowly, the glide of his lips, tongue, and teeth grazed lightly around Chase, but he couldn't maintain the slow place. Cyril needed to taste Chase's orgasm.

"Ohsweetfuck." The words came out in one breath and Chase came, crying out Cyril's name as he poured his come down Cyril's throat.

The sight of Chase's face mesmerized him. Cyril swallowed all of what he'd demanded, his tongue cleaning off Chase's cock before he drew slowly back, remaining on his knees. After several breaths to calm himself, Cyril finally found his voice. "I thought when I started all of this that the only thing I wanted was to be returned to the throne of Brenth. I was wrong. That isn't what I wanted in the end. There is something far more important to me now."

Chase leaned down and pulled Cyril to his feet. "You've asked me what I want," he said as he led Cyril over to a pile of pillows near the throne. "Now I ask you the same."

Sliding down and settling on the pillows, Cyril drew Chase with him. Bluntly honest, Cyril opened himself completely. "Everything that we had together. To follow you and Duncan wherever we might end up. Nothing else will ever mean as much to me."

Leaning over him, straddling Cyril, Chase whispered, "then take me... and let's go get our lover."

As Chase hovered over him, Cyril's hands ran lightly over his back then downward to the curve of his ass. Pulling his hand back, Cyril wet it with spit, then ran it over his own cock. "All of the above is easily arranged. My brother will take care of Brenth, and I will take care of you. Silas should have no problem, and neither will I."

Silas entered the chamber, following the mention of his name. "I should have no problem what?"

"You're giving... Oh, God..." Chase lost all semblance of speech as Cyril pushed slowly inside him.

"Well... now that's something you don't see every day," Silas commented, not appearing to be one bit surprised seeing his brother and Chase naked in the throne room. He walked toward the steps leading to the throne and sat down, getting comfortable and waiting for the other two to finish.

Staring up at Chase, Cyril whispered, "I would give up everything for you and Duncan." The slow, grinding push of his hips followed his words and he found himself lost in the plea he saw in Chase's eyes. "To see you look at me like that."

"Cyril..." Chase's head fell back, the cry low, need thrumming through him. "Love me..."

"I want you to feel how much I do." A slow tempo consumed them as Cyril deliberately kept his movements excruciatingly slow; the joining of their bodies an act of pure emotional attachment between them. Raising his head, Cyril licked at the saltiness of Chase's skin in the middle of his chest.

Chase tugged Cyril up until he was in the leader's lap, then he kissed Cyril, his arms tightening around his lover's neck as the movements sped up. "Need you. We both do."

Cyril let Chase control everything. Both of his hands caressed the captain's hips, encouraging the motion as he continued the upward grind, plunging inside Chase. Since this was the first time Cyril felt the exquisite pressure of Chase's body around his cock, he wanted it all, and he intentionally controlled the harsher surge of need trying to take him over. With a turn of his head, he whispered in Chase's ear, "Give me what I want. I want to hear you lose yourself for me, Chase."

With a deep groan, Chase rode Cyril, grinding and rocking, until the last of his control slipped. "Cyril!" Jerking hard, Chase came, his body clamping tight around Cyril's cock as his own pulsed, spilling heat between them.

The sweet sound of his name on Chase's lip sent a shudder through Cyril. He fought against coming to watch Chase's face, those eyes glazed of passion told him Chase was completely lost. Several breaths later, tremors raced through Cyril and he cried out, his body straining and burying him deep within Chase.

A strained, if somewhat amused, chuckle from the vicinity of the throne caught their attention. Chase lifted his head from where it lay on Cyril's shoulder, his eyes widening when he realized Silas was sitting there... watching them.

"Umm..."

"Now care to tell me what I have no problem with, brother?" Leaning back on both elbows, Silas eyed Cyril quizzically.

Turning his head to look over at Silas, Cyril murmured, "You should have no problem ruling Brenth."

Silas blinked as if he hadn't heard Cyril correctly. Then his eyes widened and he stared at his brother, completely flabbergasted. Gasping comically like a fish, he finally got out the words. "You want me to what?"

"I love that expression on his face," Cyril quipped before he glanced back at Chase, noticing the same look on the captain's features. Raising a brow, he eyed Chase questioningly.

"You're... you're serious," Chase whispered.

"Cyril," Silas said in an attempt to get his brother's attention.

"You thought I wasn't?" Puzzled by that attitude, Cyril stared at Chase for a long moment before Silas' attempt made him look back at his brother. "What?"

Silas opened his mouth to say something, then shut it again. The confusion had faded slightly and he ended up swallowing thickly before he tried again. "You really want me to rule Brenth?"

"You'll have my ear, brother, and my advice. But I think you are as capable as I am in this."

"Cyril." His hand on Cyril's jaw, Chase turned the ruler's head back to face him. "Are you sure this is what you want?"

Sighing quietly, Cyril shifted slightly then slipped his arms around Chase, refusing to let him go just yet. "I found something more important to me. I'd far rather lose Brenth than lose you and Duncan ever again."

Staying silent for now, Silas simply watched his brother and Chase.

Chase smiled slowly. "Then let's go get our navigator."

Chapter Twenty-Four

Duncan woke up to the darkness of the cabin and rolled onto his back. Staring at nothing, his mind felt in the same state. He'd dreamed of Eezy, and his physical reaction to the dream was extremely slow to fade. He wanted nothing more than to bury himself in that sweet ass, but it wasn't an option. The navigator hadn't cried yet about the nonsense, and he wasn't about to start now. Hauling himself up from the bed, he fumbled along the wall for the light. Tightly suppressing emotional baggage was something Duncan was good at.

Catching a look at himself in the mirror, he realized he looked like death warmed over. With an impatient run of his hand through his messed hair, he only succeeded in making it stick out at odder angles. Since he wasn't an Interferion man anymore, Duncan got a pair of jeans out of his drawer and slid them on. Who the hell needed a uniform now?

Irregardless of the fact that it felt like his life was completely in tatters, he made his way to the bridge. He didn't regret what they had done in bringing Interferion's nefarious actions to light. He only felt the loss of himself because Eezy had left. It took him a moment to notice Chase was nowhere to be seen. Figuring the captain must be working in the back bay or something, Duncan headed to the galley to brew himself a very strong pot of coffee. Except, once he was in the small kitchen, he decided to help himself to a bottle of Rin-Dart. If this didn't kill the ache in his heart and body, nothing would.

After uncapping the bottle, he tipped it up, taking several swallows as he padded back to the bridge. God, the silence was almost too much for him. To drown it out, he flipped on the com switch to the back bay. "Chase, you wanna come to the bridge?"

When only silence answered him, he stared at the console, confused. "Chase?"

Before he could begin to figure out what was going on, the alert on the stellar system started flashing red, and Mal's somber voice came over the com. "Battle cruiser, T class. Half a parsec away and closing. No frequencies open for communication."

Though the ship was cloaked, Duncan had tweaked the upgrade to Mal that gave the ship's system the ability to bypass the cloaking code. When he set the bottle down, it wobbled on the edge then fell over to the floor. Duncan ignored it as he watched the large, ominous shape on the main screen.

"Oh, fuck." He was a sitting duck just waiting to be fired on right now. Frantically, he began inputting new coordinates and arming the accelerator cells for immediate activation. Whether he could outrun a battle cruiser or not, he was about to find out.

Panic edged at his nerves but he held it back, keeping his mind level and clear. Even knowing he really didn't stand a chance in hell of out-maneuvering a class T, he'd still try. The odds weren't too heavily in favor of him, and Chase would probably be taken back to Interferion headquarters in manacles.

"What the hell is going on?" Chase's startled outburst made Duncan whirl around then freeze at the sight of CI beside Chase. It registered that Silas and Vilichr were standing beside them, but the only thing Duncan saw was Cyril. For a moment, his emotions took a hold of him and lay bare in his eyes; the next his heart dropped. If the command on the battle cruiser realized CI was on this ship, they would kill him.

"Oh God, you've got to get him out of here." Abruptly, Duncan turned back to the console to link the deflector probe to the small cruiser that was docked to the ship.

When nobody moved behind him, Duncan yelled, "They'll kill him! Get CI out of here!"

Suddenly, the large battle cruiser appeared on the bridge screen and the sight galvanized Chase into action. He ran over to the console and activated the ship's outer shields.

"They're arming up, Captain." Mal's voice came over the computer com.

"Signal them! Tell them we surrender!" Duncan screamed the order at Mal before Vilichr stepped forward and shoved him to the side.

"Mal, open a channel, code seven seven one."

When the startled face of the commander of the battle cruiser appeared on the screen, Duncan backed up, trying to shield Cyril from view.

"Stand down. I order you to stand down immediately," Vilichr barked.

"Ambassador Kralycy?" Confused, the commander's mouth opened like a fish gasping for air.

Straightening from the console to ensure he could be seen on the two-way screen, Vilichr gave his orders again. "Stand down immediately."

"We've orders to fire on the renegades' ship, Ambassador."

Both Duncan and Chase were doing their best to keep Cyril shielded from sight behind them. Duncan had tried to edge Cyril toward the corridor and out of the bridge, but CI wasn't budging. His fingers laced with Duncan's, refusing to relinquish his hold on the navigator.

Duncan didn't say anything, but he knew if the commander saw CI, he would completely disregard whoever else was on the ship and fire on it. The only thing on Duncan's mind was getting Cyril to safety.

"Disregard. Top priority, Bravo eight twelve dash three Foxtrot. Stand down now. I have control of this situation." With a fierce look, Vilichr stared down the commander until the man looked away.

"Standing down now."

When the image of the commander faded to a black screen, Duncan slumped back against Cyril in relief. He didn't even realize he'd begun trembling.

Chase rushed to Duncan and cupped his navigator's face. Without saying a word, he kissed his lover hard, pinning Duncan between himself and Cyril.

Normally Duncan might have reacted differently, but he was completely dazed. A low groan escaped him and he parted his lips to the captain, arms snaking around Chase's neck, holding on tight.

"Please," Chase whispered across Duncan's lips. "Give him a chance, love."

Stiffening slightly at the reminder, Duncan drew back, his features a bland mask. "If the commander would have seen him, CI would have automatically been a dead man. So why is he here?"

Chase looked up at Cyril and sighed. "Because he... I... we can't just throw away what we had, Duncan. Don't you see?

He had no choice to do what he did. Yes, it pissed me off to find out that we'd been used, but do you really think falling in love was part of his plan?" He cupped Duncan's cheek gently, lowering his voice. "Do you really think it was part of our plan?"

Cyril slid out from behind Duncan and walked to the com. Sitting in the captain's chair, he stared out into the empty space visible on the screen.

"So we forgive him. Fine." Glancing briefly at Cyril, Duncan gave him a strained smile. "You're forgiven, all right? Now you can go home happy. And I think we need to get out of here before the commander of that battle cruiser decides to change his mind."

Moving toward the console, Duncan began setting a new course to take advantage of the temporary reprieve Vilichr had gotten them.

Chase stormed over to the chair and jerked it around. Before he could land the slap to Duncan's face, however, another hand shot out, clasping Chase's arm. Chase looked up at Cyril. Cyril didn't say a word, just released Chase, tugged Duncan right out of the chair, and slammed him against the hull, kissing him hard enough to bruise.

More shock than anything held Duncan rigid. Even as he fought the feelings attempting to overwhelm him, he began to fail. The hungry, demanding touch of Cyril's mouth couldn't silence the pained whimper rising in Duncan. He'd dreamed of Cyril and wanted him beyond his own ability to control.

Silently, Vilichr took over the duties of navigating the ship and Silas helped him.

"You can run from me forever," Cyril whispered gruffly, "but I will follow you everywhere, Duncan. I won't go on without you."

Confused, Duncan could think of no clear reason why CI would even bother. Silently studying his face, Duncan didn't say anything for a long time. He could see the emotions on CI's face and knew they mirrored his own. Yet it wasn't enough and probably never would be. "I don't think you have a choice unless you plan on putting us in your harem."

Glancing over Cyril's shoulder toward Chase, he really didn't think even his partner would go for that.

Defeat was the only emotion remaining on Cyril's face. Stepping back, he released Duncan. "I see." He turned and started for the door leading out of the bridge.

In two quick strides, Chase had Duncan's shirt bunched in his fists. "He fucked up, so the punishment is to break his heart?" he hissed.

Staring in shock at Chase, Duncan was left speechless. It required a moment for Duncan to get his brain to function enough to form the words. Starting to get pissed as well, Duncan didn't know what the hell was going on. "Punishment? What the hell are you talking about?"

"He gave up the throne for us!" Chase shouted, releasing Duncan abruptly. "It's gone, Duncan! He gave up everything for us."

Duncan really didn't like Chase screaming at him and acting like he'd done something seriously wrong. When Vilichr moved away from the console to lay a calming hand on Duncan's shoulder, the ambassador's eyes narrowed on Chase since the captain wasn't handling things very well. A quiet whisper in Duncan's ear caused the navigator's stormy expression to fade.

Chase spun on his heel and left the bridge, hurrying after Cyril.

Why was he left feeling like he was the one who'd done something wrong? Duncan hadn't known Cyril that gave up his throne, and it seemed like nobody cared to listen to him at this point. His first instinct had been to run after both of them, but from Chase's parting expression, Duncan didn't think he'd be welcome. Moving toward his chair, he sat down heavily.

"Duncan." Silas knelt in front of him. "Please... listen to me. Cyril turned the throne of Brenth over to me. He hasn't been himself since... since he left you. He has hardly eaten a thing, finds no joy in the company of anyone else. He loves you, Duncan, both of you. Dearly."

Staring helplessly at Silas, all Duncan could do was listen to him. "Is that why he gave up the throne?"

"He gave it up for you," Vilichr said, laying a hand on Duncan's shoulder. "You both mean more to him than anything in this universe."

Given a chance to absorb that fact, Duncan stood and helped Silas up. "I think I need to talk to Cyril."

Releasing Silas, he gave both of them a strained smile before he walked out of the bridge. On the outer wall, he pressed the button to turn on the ship scan in order to find CI. Locating him and Chase both in the back bay, he hesitated briefly. Finally, he shut off the scan and headed for the bay doors.

Chase was sitting with his back to the door, head cradled in his hands. "I'm so sorry," he whispered. "I thought…" He shook his head.

"I'm sorry, too." Cyril knelt down beside him. "I never meant to hurt either of you. I never meant to fall in love."

Duncan stopped near the doorway, listening to the two of them. His gaze traveled over Cyril then Chase, studying the two men who meant more to him than his own life. "I'm not so sure you were very wise in giving up your throne, Cyril."

Cyril stood slowly, patting Chase's back. "It was my choice. Humans are not the only ones to use their hearts over their heads."

"We all make mistakes, Cyril. I know that with the best of them." After taking a few slow steps toward him, Duncan stilled completely. "I've wanted you back ever since you left."

Swallowing, Cyril closed his eyes. "I can't live without you," he said quietly.

"You don't have to." Closing the distance between them, Duncan reached for Cyril and drew him close. Pressing a soft kiss to CI's lips, he whispered, "Kiss me as you once did. Like I belong to you."

It had taken Duncan a very long time to understand the meaning of that first kiss, but now he finally did.

Cyril opened his eyes and met Duncan's gaze. "Duncan…" He gave Duncan no chance to respond, just took him in a desperate, soul-consuming kiss, holding nothing back.

One hand reached out blindly for his husband as Duncan clung to Cyril, letting his senses fill with the taste he'd come to need. A low whimper began in his throat as his free hand wrapped tightly within Cyril's hair, holding him right where he was.

Vilichr's frantic voice came over the com. "We need you on the bridge, we have a problem."

The urgent tone broke Duncan and Cyril's kiss. Chase grabbed Duncan's hand and they ran back to the bridge, Cyril following behind. The moment Duncan saw the view of the battle cruiser back on the main screen, he knew they were really in trouble. Reacting in a split second, he stepped back and pushed Cyril hard to the side, out of range of the com camera.

"You've been ordered to stand down. Top priority, Bravo eight twelve dash three Foxtrot." Vilichr repeated his order to the commander of the ship then fell silent when the enraged face of President Xere appeared on the screen.

"Either hand over the traitors, or we will fire on your ship."

Angrily, Vilichr shot back, "You have no authority, Xere."

"Fuck," Duncan muttered under his breath and strode toward the console. He began keying in the information to activate the Exodus chip transporter code. He was the only one, besides CI, who knew the chip he'd installed for Mal also contained the Brenth coordinates code.

"You son of a bitch." Chase stepped forward to engage the ship's shields and sent out a frantic message to Arch at Interferion.

There was little likelihood of them surviving sustained blasts from the battle cruiser for long. Both Duncan and Chase knew it. Turning to face Vilichr, Chase's tone was urgent. "Let them take us and you three get the hell out of here."

"Silas, send a dispatch to General Kalmer. Order the Eighth Fleet to this sector." When CI stepped into view, the expression on Xere's face became downright comical as it turned completely red. Xere's mouth dropped open and his breath came in short, sharp gasps.

"Mal, on my order engage code on screen. Tac positions four humanoids." Rapidly Duncan typed in the sequence of numbers needed to start the transporter module. Unfortunately, it could only handle four bodies at a time.

"Fire to disable that ship. I wanted it boarded and everyone taken prisoner." Xere directed his order to someone out of sight of the com camera. The ex-president's shock had rapidly become an exultant glee as he stared at CI.

When Cyril saw the flash of numbers displayed on the screen, he half turned toward Duncan. As if he knew what the navigator was doing, a frightened look crossed his features. "No, Duncan... stop. There won't be time for all of us."

Before anybody could say anything else, Mal announced, "Main transporter on Brenth linked. Code accepted."

Automatically, the ship had to drop its shield and Chase, Cyril, Vilichr, and Silas disappeared in the transporter field. In the next second, a blast from the cruiser hit the outer hull and the ship shook violently, sending Duncan flying back against the console. The use of the transporter had drained a good portion of the ship's energy, but there should be just enough for one last transport. Regaining his wits, Duncan scrambled to his feet and tried to reenter the code, but it was already too late. When he heard the heavy thud of the guards running toward the bridge, he hastily deleted the code with a push of a button then destroyed the chip.

"Find the others!" An irate voice screamed as several hands grabbed Duncan and yanked him back from the console.

Duncan struggled against the men who held him, but it was useless and he was jerked around to face Xere.

The ex-president looked in danger of an apoplectic fit. "Where is CI?"

Another guard entered the bridge and addressed Xere. "Nobody else is here, President Xere."

"Where are they, Sampson?" Taking hold of Duncan's arms, Xere began shaking the navigator. Bringing his hands up, Duncan struck at Xere's arms, breaking the hold. When he tried to grab for Xere's throat, the other men dragged him back.

"You're not—" Duncan wasn't given the chance to finish. With a hard blow to the back of his head, starbursts exploded in his mind and he dropped to the floor.

* * *

Blinding white walls made Duncan's head hurt even more when he opened his eyes.

"What's the transporter code into Brenth?"

A moment passed before Duncan could focus on the face asking the question. The blur cleared and he saw Xere settled in a chair near him, smiling unpleasantly. When Duncan tried to move, he found he couldn't. He'd been strapped down to the bed.

"Wouldn't do you any good to know, Xere. You don't have the Exodus chip."

The smile on Xere's lips widened and was no less unpleasant as he raised his hand. Between his fingers, he held a crysta-film wrapped chip. "Now what is the code, Sampson?"

Staring silently at the chip, Duncan realized his own position in an instant, but still he wouldn't talk. He'd forgotten about the second chip he'd taken and did his best to hide the dismay he felt. If he could find a way to speak to somebody on the ship, he could tell them Xere had been ousted from his position. It was more than obvious Xere had held back a battalion for the emergency he found himself in. If the commander of the ship found out Xere was a renegade, the ex-president would be the one clapped in irons.

Xere seemed to have no problem at all talking; if anything, he had trouble hiding his cheerful glee. "One strike would be all it would take. A select platoon assassinating CI and Interferion is back at the helm of Brenth."

"You're fucking crazy."

"No, I'm the one with the chip and you. And instead of killing you as I originally planned, you'll be my special guest on Vius."

Shit. Duncan knew if they made it to Lymusiadus prison, he'd never get out of there, dead or alive. Struggling to free himself from the straps restraining him, Duncan barely felt the sting of a needle inserted into his arm.

"Since I don't want you talking to my crew, you'll sleep until Talos is ready to play with you."

Even though Duncan didn't like the sound of that, there wasn't anything he could do as he slipped into unconsciousness.

When next he opened his eyes Duncan didn't have a headache. However, he was naked and hanging in chains, so it definitely wasn't an improvement.

Xere sat in his chair nearby, relaxing as he ate dinner. "Good thing you woke up. Talos has been getting impatient."

The only other person in the room grinned at Duncan, showing blackened and missing teeth. Duncan would have noticed more if it weren't for the vicious-looking whip in Talos' hand.

"One last chance, Sampson. Give me the code, and you're free." Glancing over at Talos, Xere smirked as he continued. "Once Talos starts, he really hates to stop."

"Sorry, can't really remember it." It was the only answer Xere would get out of Duncan.

"That's not what I want to hear." In an indolent gesture, Xere motioned Talos to begin.

No punches pulled, the first strike to Duncan's flesh drew blood. The navigator had to grit his teeth tightly with the torture of torn flesh.

"Once I've taken care of CI permanently, Oera will be returned to the throne." Settling back in his seat, Xere savored his glass of wine, seemingly in his own fantasy world. "I'm really looking forward to squashing that annoying bug."

Pain became agony under the relentless pattern of the whip to Duncan's skin. Rhythmic thuds accompanied the drone of Xere's voice, plotting his great comeback at Interferion. At some point, the navigator could no longer control his reactions to the overwhelming sensation of multiple lacerations, and he began screaming.

Talos stepped back with a pleased grin as Xere approached Duncan. Stepping around Duncan, Talos' grimy hand brushed back the sweat-matted hair from Duncan's eyes.

"You're losing quite a bit of blood there, Sampson. But don't worry, Talos will keep you alive. Anything you want to tell me? You might want to give me what I want to know before he begins the next step. You really won't like it."

Duncan stared back at him, dull eyes barely registering the sight of the two. Still he managed to shake his head, refusing to give in.

"It's your body." With a shrug, Xere motioned Talos to continue.

After placing the whip on a table, Talos picked up a large jar and opened it. "This will take care of you real good. It won't feel good cuz I added an irritant, but at least you'll stop bleeding. Then I'll work on you again."

As he slathered the thick glob of the lotion over the cuts on Duncan's back, it had the effect of salt poured on open wounds. Duncan's body shook violently, trying to get away from the pain as he screamed. The feeling had taken over Duncan's mind and there was no place for him to escape the agonizing fire.

The taste of a bitter liquid flooded Duncan's mouth and he choked on it. As Talos forced more down his throat, Duncan had no choice but to drink it.

Chapter Twenty-Five

"Fewver, is the Eighth Fleet at the last known position of Interferion 7334?"

Looking up from his screen, the lieutenant said, "Yes, CI. But there's no sign of either the battle cruiser or the other ship. There's a field of debris and Commandant Kalmer verified its part of Interferion 212."

Agitated, Cyril turned to the man at the console next to him. "Any ideas where that damn battalion is?"

"There's no signature in the sub space field. We're widening the scan to a thousand parsecs right now."

Chase stood next to Cyril, his hand tightly clasped around CI's. He couldn't help showing the worry on his expression. He wasn't sure if Xere had killed Duncan outright or not. All around the military council room, several of Cyril's officers were working at their stations.

"Commandant Kalmer is holding position until we receive verification of the battle cruiser's whereabouts. If Xere shows up, it won't take long for the fleet to get to him."

"CI, message coming through from Star Commander Arch Fredericks."

"Put it through, Vart." His patience wearing thin, Cyril began pacing as Arch appeared on the huge screen over the main console. "How in the hell did Xere get a battalion?"

"He's managed to rotate several different squadrons on lockdown operations over the last year. The commanders of the ships aren't aware Xere is now a renegade. They are operating on normal lockdown procedure." Arch looked extremely tired, as if he hadn't slept in a week. "None of us were aware of his contingency plan until he forced the confrontation with Chase and Duncan."

"He's got Duncan, Arch." Chase stepped forward. "Where in the hell is he? Any ideas?"

"We've got techs trying to override the communications signals, but so far no luck. None of our contacts at Xere's known places of operation are coming up with anything. Until he comes out of hiding, we don't know where he is."

Feeling helpless and useless, Chase slammed his fist against the nearest wall. "We've got to find him."

"Three battalions are being sent to join the Eighth Fleet. We'll find him, Chase, I swear." Though Arch's tone was weary, a thread of determination ran through the words. "Orders are to execute Xere on sight."

"Do your best, Arch." The outburst of rage from Chase had the effect of temporarily calming Cyril down. Arch's image faded from the screen as Cyril walked over to Chase. "We will get him back. Even if I have to tear apart the entire Ura-tet galaxy."

Enfolding Chase in his arms, Cyril held tightly to him. Chase buried his face against Cyril's throat, trying to stop the scalding hot tears from falling. He didn't know where his husband was, didn't know what was happening to Duncan.

Fewver looked up from the readout of his com screen. Puzzled, he cleared his throat then hesitated. Eyeing him back, Cyril lifted his head and his brow rose questioningly.

"CI, there's an incoming message for Chase Sykes from Rudolpho Bernard." His tone lowered uncertainly on the name since everybody knew the notorious underworld trader.

Releasing CI, Chase moved rapidly toward the main com screen. "Put him on."

The moment Rudy appeared, he said, "Heard there'd been some trouble, Chase, and I figured you'd need some help. Especially since my sources tell me Xere has Duncan imprisoned at Lymusiadus."

"He's still alive." Hearing the news, relief warred with the fury and eased the fear in Chase.

"CI, Lymusiadus is too heavily fortified for the Eighth Fleet to do any good in the immediate future. It would take months to break through," Vart said.

"I can get somebody in for you, but it can't be either you or Cyril. Your faces are too well known." Rudy made the offer without even flinching.

Completely caught off guard, both Cyril and Chase stared at him in amazement. When the silence stretched on a bit too long, Rudy shrugged like it was no big deal. "Eh, I owe you one. You have no idea of how well I made out on broadcasting the news you left me."

Frowning in concentration, Chase tried to figure out who they could send in. Somebody that he would trust, somebody that wouldn't be recognized from the daily news broadcasts sent out by Interferion. When it came to him, he grabbed hold of Cyril's hand. "Iari, King of Iceu. Both Chase and I know him, and I believe you do, too."

Thoughtfully, Cyril nodded. "He'd get in and out and leave quite a few bodies behind." Turning away from Chase, he gave the order. "Andel, send a request to Iceu requesting King Iari come to the Universal Palace."

Hastily typing, Andel nodded. "Outgoing now, CI."

"I can get two people into Lymusiadus. Let me see what else I can come up with on my end," Rudy said. "It won't take Iari long to arrive, and I should be right behind him." Without waiting for them to say anything, Rudy cut the com connection and disappeared from the screen.

For the first time, Chase felt hopeful since he'd realized Duncan wasn't behind them when they transported to Brenth. When he looked at Cyril, he saw the same emotion reflected in the smoke-gray eyes. "We'll have him back soon, Cyril."

"It's driving me crazy, Chase. I can't even imagine what Xere could be doing to him. I'm trying to be patient, but..."

"It's hell, I know." Squeezing Cyril's hand, Chase pulled him closer.

They both realized exactly why Xere would be keeping Duncan alive. Duncan obviously had the transport code for Brenth. Something Xere would probably do anything to get his hands on. The security in the palace was held at high alert for the time being. In his thoughts, Chase tried to send a quiet message to Duncan. *Hold on love, we'll be there soon.* Pulling back slightly, Chase stared silently at Cyril. It seemed like a very long time ago that they'd discovered Eezy was CI, but it had only been a week. With a soft whisper, Chase released him.

"We love you."

"I love both of you as well," Cyril answered.

Because they needed to make the plans necessary to take over Lymusiadus, neither of them had but that moment to hold onto one another. After they parted, Cyril began coordinating a plan for his military fleet to get as close to Vius as they could without being detected. When Iari and Rudy arrived, Chase worked with them on getting into the prison and getting

Duncan out. Once that was achieved, the combined forces of Brenth, Interferion, and several others would force a surrender on Vius no matter how long it took.

* * *

"Duncan."

The navigator heard the sound of his name, but it seemed far away. Unfortunately, the darkness he'd succumb to had begun to fade from his senses, bringing back the agonizing ravages of his body.

"Duncan, wake up." This time his name was spoken louder, and he thought he recognized the voice. It required a great deal of effort to open his eyes. "Nerk?"

"Hold him while I get the chains unfastened." Another familiar voice intruded and Duncan thought he was hallucinating.

"We probably don't have much time, Iari." Trying to hold Duncan as gently as he could, Nerk kept the navigator still.

The shift of his body sent more waves of pain through Duncan, but he couldn't even scream. His throat was already raw and he wasn't sure how long he'd been tortured, or when his voice had given out. As they moved him, Duncan caught a brief glimpse of Xere and Talos, lying unconscious or dead on the floor.

When the shackles were taken off, Duncan almost collapsed, unable to bear his own weight. Both of the men caught him before he could hit the floor. Trying not to slip on the blood pooled on the stone, Iari carefully picked Duncan up.

The harsh sound of a siren wailed through the building, startling them all. "Fuck, somebody triggered the alarm," Iari hissed.

"Just take care of him. I'll slow down anybody getting in here." Nerk rushed off to the one lone door that led into the room. Pulling a Welder Wand from his jacket pocket, he turned it on and began melting the metal frame of the door to seal the room. It would give them the time they needed to set up and activate the DP Gateway.

Duncan, wavering in and out of conscious, only caught disjointed pieces of what was going on. Iari carried him to the closest table and carefully put him down, then the king began searching through the bottles and jars near him. After picking up several, he sniffed at their contents then threw them on the floor.

"God of Pleras, isn't there anything in this place to heal him. He'll bleed to death before we can get out of here."

Once he'd gotten the door welded shut, Nerk hurried toward the center of the room to set up the transporter gateway. "Do the best you can. I'll have this ready in a few minutes. I don't think we have much longer than that."

The banging on the outer door was near deafening, but hopefully it would hold until they could get out of there.

Picking up a large black jar, Iari smelled the odor of Alumnel and Titerasen. "This would stop the bleeding, but..." He trailed off, uncertain if he should take the chance. Already his tunic was soaked with Duncan's blood and the hideous wounds were still bleeding.

Knowing he had no choice, he scooped out a handful of the grease and smoothed it over the worst of the damage.

Duncan's body strained off the table, convulsing as he screamed. The white heat of the pain drove out the blackness of unconsciousness, leaving him awash in the internal fire burning him.

Startled, Nerk stopped for a moment, staring wide-eyed at Iari as the king struggled to hold Duncan down. Rushing to get the circuit operational, Nerk inserted the code and location chip. Once they'd been transported, the gateway would self-destruct.

When Duncan collapsed back onto the table, the screams faded to no more than pained whimpers. Leaving him alone for a moment, Iari went to take care of Xere. He had no qualms about what he was going to do. The prone body of the ex-president didn't even stir as the king approached.

Pulling out his laser sword from its sheath, the king leaned down and grabbed a handful of Xere's hair. Groaning as his eyes opened, Xere didn't even have a chance to react other than a piercing scream that abruptly stopped when Iari's blade sliced through his neck. Detaching the head from the body, he left Xere's carcass flopping on the floor. The heat of the blade had cauterized the skin and he dropped the head into a large bag.

Nerk seemed unmoved as he finished working on the gateway. "It's ready, Iari."

After tossing the bag to Nerk, Iari went back to the table and picked up Duncan as gently as he could. The navigator's eyelids fluttered open and tried to focus on the king.

"I've got you, Duncan. Everything is all right." The quiet voice soothed through the navigator as Duncan passed out in Iari's arms.

Iari and Nerk stepped into the portal then. A blinding brilliance surrounded them and when it cleared, they were standing in the TR room on Brenth.

Cyril and Chase froze, staring at the body in Iari's arms. For a moment, neither of them could move, but then Cyril began issuing orders to his servants. "Call every one of the royal doctors to the infirmary. Signal Commander Kalmer to base for now."

As the captain took Duncan from him, Iari said, "Silas, take them down to the infirmary. I need to speak to Cyril."

Rudolpho stepped forward, inspecting his son for a long moment. Then he broke out in a smile when he found no damage. Iari stood beside Nerk and signaled Cyril to move closer. "Xere has been taken care of, Cyril. I should have brought him back, but seeing what Xere did to him, I was too angry."

Nerk lifted the bag, showing it to CI. Cyril glanced at the bag, realizing what was probably in it. He glanced back at the king. "I understand, Iari. I would have killed him on the spot as well."

Turning to look at Rudolpho and Nerk, Cyril managed a smile, though he really didn't feel particularly happy. Still, both men deserved his gratitude for what they had done. "You have the thanks of Brenth for aiding us in getting Duncan back. Please accept our hospitality and remain here as long as you want. I will see to it you are given a very suitable reward."

"A small yearly allotment of Adasanef and Mevapa?" Rudolpho suggested hopefully, and Nerk rolled his eyes as he handed the bag over to Cyril.

Cyril couldn't help but laugh. Obviously the underworld trader always had his eye to the main chance. "We shall see about that."

Pleased with himself, Rudolpho took hold of his son and they both left the chamber. As Cyril turned to Iari, the king hastily made his way out the door. "I'll just go do what I'm supposed to do."

The small moment of humor was lost to the worry of his thoughts as Cyril headed down to the infirmary. The place was a hive of activity with personnel going in and out of the royal suite. Seeing Chase standing by the door, trying to look in every time the door opened, Cyril handed the bag in his hand to one of his servants then approached the captain. He took Chase by the arm and drew him away.

"I have the finest doctors on Brenth in there, Chase. They'll take care of him. I promise."

"I've tried to calm him, but I'm not doing much good." Silas brought up his hands in a helpless gesture.

"You'll need to handle the incoming messages from Interferion, Silas. Go back to the throne room and take your place." Though it wasn't an order, Cyril knew Silas needed to be at the helm, directing everything.

"Let me know, all right?" Silas looked at him over his shoulder as he headed toward the outer doors.

Cyril nodded and slipped his arm around Chase, turning his attention to the captain. But it seemed Chase couldn't be still. He pulled away from Cyril and began pacing in front of the infirmary door.

Iari entered the room and sighed heavily, watching both of them. "Xere worked him over pretty bad."

"If you hadn't killed him, I would have." Cyril waved away one of the servants trying to hover near him. Eyeing the blood-stained clothing Iari was still wearing, he added, "Why don't you go get cleaned up and get some rest? I'll let you know what the doctors say when they come out."

Another heavy sigh accompanied Iari's nod. "I think we're all due for a vacation after this."

"What he must have gone through." Chase was too worried to keep his thoughts to himself.

When the king moved toward the captain, Cyril waved him off. "Go get some sleep, Iari. That's an order."

Reluctantly, Iari turned away and left the room.

"I want to be in there with him, damn it." Frustrated and angry, Chase took it out on the nearest wall and only ended up damaging his hand.

"We need to let the doctors do their work, Chase." Subduing his own anxiety, Cyril moved toward him and grabbed his arm. He turned the captain around and pulled him close. Chase clung to him, swallowing back his tears.

Several servants remained near them but didn't dare interrupt. Cyril and Chase ignored them as they held tightly to one another.

"I can't even imagine, Cyril." Chase nearly choked getting out the words.

"It's over now and he's safe. As soon as we can, we'll leave here. Just the three of us." Cyril caressed Chase's hair.

One of the doctors emerged from the royal suite. Both Cyril and Chase stilled completely when they saw him. Cyril found his voice first. "Is he all right?"

"Can we see him?" Chase's question followed Cyril's. When he moved to take a step forward, Cyril held him back.

"Yes to both questions. We managed to stabilize him. He's pretty incoherent at the moment, but he'll be awake for a short time."

When he let go of Chase, the captain hurried through the inner room doors and Cyril followed him, listening to the doctor.

"There was a great deal of damage, CI. We've stopped the bleeding and have begun treatments with the Responsive Cell Analyzer. He'll be on the Embedded Dream System to keep the memories at bay while his body heals. In this case, I don't think we have much of a choice."

The moment Chase saw Duncan, he hurried toward the bed and settled on the edge of it, taking hold of the navigator's hand. Cyril stopped in dismay, seeing the Duncan's wrapped body. The binding cloth protected the wounds from any form of contamination, and they made the navigator look like an ancient Egyptian mummy.

When Duncan's eyes opened, Cyril joined Chase with a light laugh. "Well, now don't you look all dressed up with no place to go?"

"That worried, are you?" A lopsided grin answered Cyril as Duncan looked between them, but it appeared he had some trouble focusing on them.

"If you weren't in this bed, I'd be beating your ass. That's for sure." Chase lifted the hand to his lips, pressing several soft kisses to the back of it. They were both doing their best to hide their worry from Duncan.

Cyril sat on the other side of the bed, reaching out to smooth his hand gently over Duncan's hair. "We both would be."

"CI, we can have him moved upstairs if you wish. It would be easier than having the two of you living in the infirmary." Amused, the doctor waited silently for Cyril's order.

"That would be best. See to it, Halfour."

"You're stuck in this bed until we tell you to move. Now how good is that?" A wicked grin curved Chase's lip as he lowered Duncan's hand but kept hold of it.

"Umm, my idea of paradise." The drowsy sound of Duncan's voice faded over the last word as the navigator fell asleep.

Chapter Twenty-Six

Eezy lazed on the fur rug in front of the fireplace. Stretched out on his side, he stared into the dancing flames. The heat warmed through him as he waited for Chase to finish fixing dinner.

When Duncan came from the back hall, Eezy motioned to him. "Chase won't let us into the kitchen. He wants dinner to be a surprise."

With a nod, Duncan changed direction and headed toward Eezy. Eezy's eyes traveled over the body clad only in a pair of loose cotton pants. All three of them had gone completely casual and relaxed once they'd arrived on Duncan's planet two days ago. They'd been at pains to forget everything that had happened, mostly for Duncan's sake.

With a quiet sigh, Duncan sat down beside Eezy. The sight laid out on the fur rug was temptation itself. Though the doctor's orders had forbidden any activity other than short walks, Duncan's attempts to control his own wayward impulses were being strained to the limit.

Rolling onto his side, Eezy held out a hand to Duncan. "How are you feeling, love?" he asked as he eased Duncan down beside him.

Twining his fingers with Eezy's, Duncan laid them against his side. "I'm feeling absolutely fucking great. Not one problem."

One eyebrow rose and Eezy shifted until he was hovering over Duncan, careful not to put any weight on him. "I know that tone." He stroked Duncan's jawline with his fingertips, brushing them slowly over Duncan's lips. "I know you're going stir-crazy, but it won't be like this forever. What can I do to help?"

Duncan tried to arch upward toward Eezy. More than anything, he wanted to feel the reality of what had been haunting his dreams. Raising his head, he whispered against Eezy's lips, "Fuck me. Just fuck me."

Eezy stilled, breath catching. "Duncan..." He pulled back enough to see Duncan's eyes. His gaze not leaving Duncan's, Eezy trailed his fingers down Duncan's neck, over his chest, to circle one nipple. "I can't, babe." Before Duncan could speak, Eezy leaned down and flicked Duncan's nipple with his tongue. "But I can do something else, provided you promise not to move."

Whether or not he was in pain afterwards didn't matter to Duncan, and he wanted a hell of a lot more than just that. A gasp escaped him with the teasing of Eezy's touch. "I'm going to want more. I want you, damn it."

"You've got me," Eezy murmured, releasing Duncan's nipple. He slithered down Duncan's body, lips and tongue stroking every bit of skin he could. Hooking his fingers in the waistband of Duncan's pants, Eezy worked them down and off. "Fuck, you're beautiful." He parted Duncan's legs gently and slid back up between them.

Reaching out, Duncan tried to caress every inch of Eezy he could. He needed desperately to feel something beside the bouts of pain he was still heavily medicated against.

Rolling his eyes to look at Duncan, Eezy swallowed Duncan's cock, nose burying into the curls at the base. One hand cupped Duncan's balls, rolling them gently, tugging enough for Duncan to feel it. Eezy's other hand snaked up to pinch at Duncan's right nipple, twisting it slightly.

The sensation sent the ache inside of Duncan skyrocketing and though he tried to still the movement of his hips, he couldn't. With a deep groan, he gave into the urge to fuck Eezy's mouth, and he wanted to feel more. After catching Eezy's hand, Duncan guided it further down toward his ass.

Eezy let go of Duncan's nipple and caught his hip, pinning Duncan to the floor. He pulled back up Duncan's cock, rolling his tongue around the flared head before sucking on the tip. He let it slip out of his mouth and sucked on two fingers to wet them, then he pushed them slowly into Duncan.

"Don't move," he warned. Then he dipped his head down and caught Duncan's cock again, the suction strong as his fingers curled forward to stroke over Duncan's gland.

Turning his head slightly, Duncan saw Chase standing in the doorway, staring at them. When Duncan reached out toward him, Chase moved forward, settling at Duncan's head. As one of his hands smoothed over Duncan's chest beside Eezy, Duncan moaned low in his throat. He wanted and needed both of them. It had been too long since they'd truly been together. Desperation tinged Duncan's expression as he tried his damnedest not to move.

"Love you," Chase whispered before catching Duncan's lips in a deep kiss. Eezy's hand drifted back up to twine his fingers with Chase's, their hands resting on Duncan's stomach. "Come on, love." Chase licked Duncan's lips as Eezy began working Duncan's cock in earnest.

More than the physical enveloped Duncan. Chase and Eezy were his world and their love was the stability that kept

Duncan sane. Allowing himself to drift within the sensation of his own body, he returned Chase's kiss with a needful one of his own. It didn't take long for it to become too much for Duncan, and his body strained hard, keeping him buried in Eezy's mouth as he came. His cry was taken by Chase, muffled by the hard press of his lips.

Eezy swallowed, then licked him clean. Shifting to the other side of Duncan, Eezy joined them in the kiss, all three mouths and tongues tangling together. Both Eezy and Chase were hard, cocks pressing on Duncan's hips.

"God, I've missed this," Eezy murmured.

After catching his breath, Duncan smiled lazily at them. The painkillers still kept the harsher twinges at bay, but it was catching up to Duncan. He just refused to show it right then. "Think I can watch the floor show, too?"

Eezy chuckled as he ran his hand along Chase's hip. Eyeing Chase with a questioning look, the grin on his lips widened. "I like the idea. What about you?"

Chase rose up and answered with a hard kiss to Eezy's lips. Looking down at Duncan, he smiled slowly. "What exactly do you want to see?"

"I want to see you making love to him, Chase." If Duncan wasn't allowed to enjoy the real thing, at least he could watch the other two.

More than happy to oblige, Eezy stretched out on the fur rug. "You might want to either get the lube or make use of my mouth."

Chase grinned and held up a tube. "Way ahead of you." He kissed Duncan again and crawled over him to kneel between Eezy's legs. Giving Duncan a wink, Chase lifted Eezy's legs, pushing them up as he settled down. Then he dove in, tongue flicking over the puckered hole before pushing inside.

"Oh, fuck..." Eezy's eyes rolled back, finally closing as he groaned. He held his legs for Chase, hips bucking slightly, fucking himself on Chase's tongue. "Chase. Babe."

Rolling to his side, Duncan moved downward to get a better view of the other two. The sight of his husband's tongue sinking into Eezy's ass fascinated him. Sooner or later, he'd convince both of them to do the same thing to him, and probably a hell of a lot sooner than later. Laying his hand on Eezy's hip, Duncan ran his fingers over the warm skin, feeling the rolling movement and the shiver of Eezy's body.

Picking up the lube from where Chase had tossed it, Duncan squirted some out on his hand as his foot nudged Chase to roll slightly to the side. Once Chase's cock was exposed, Duncan patiently applied the gel, slicking it slowly over Chase.

"Please," Eezy pleaded.

Chase surged upward, impaling Eezy on his cock in one smooth motion as he took Eezy's mouth. Knees anchored on the floor, he started thrusting—hard and deep. Eezy's fingers dug into Chase's shoulders, his cries muffled in the kiss.

Duncan raised up on his elbow, fingers sliding between the crack of Chase's ass before plunging inward. He could still participate, and the rub of his fingers nailed Chase's prostate each time Chase pushed into Eezy. Wrapping his legs around Chase, Eezy rocked hard against him, intensifying the friction for both of them.

"Fuck!" Chase tore from the kiss, groaning with every rock between Eezy and Duncan. "Don't stop, Duncan," he gasped, movements quickening.

Sliding his hands down, Eezy held Chase open for Duncan. He arched into every thrust, panting as Chase drove them both harder.

Eezy lost it first, the wild gyration of his body straining against Chase's. Crying out sharply, he clung to Chase, bucking beneath him.

Deliberately, Duncan quickened the torturous rub within Chase's body as he watched Eezy's expression. The sight of the two men he loved most in the middle of their own passion was a fucking hot image.

"Duncan!" Chase jerked and slammed into Eezy, shuddering out his release. A few seconds later, he slumped, breath pushing out of his lungs in quick bursts. He moaned slightly and rocked back onto Duncan's fingers.

Slowing the internal pressure, Duncan still kept his fingers buried in Chase's ass. Though he knew what Chase wanted, Duncan's energy level wasn't quite up to par. Carefully shifting closer to him, Duncan leaned down and whispered, "Later tonight, when I can."

The look on Duncan's face showed he wouldn't accept any arguments to the contrary about what he wanted.

Eezy looked up at him then over at Chase. Giving Chase an uncertain look, he wasn't sure how to handle Duncan's increasing determination. Both of them had struggled with keeping Duncan from overdoing anything, and Duncan knew it.

"I suppose arguing is out of the question," Chase said, pursing his lips in mock frustration.

Snorting, Eezy slid out from under him and stood. "We're talking about Duncan," he said, inching his way backward, a smile just barely breaking through. "You really have to ask?"

Since he couldn't take his pain pills until after dinner, Duncan had to put up with nauseous twinges in his body, but he refused to let anything show as he carefully got up.

Eezy grabbed Duncan's hand, helping him to stand. He shot a look at Chase but didn't say anything.

Chase sighed and stood, bracing Duncan on the other side. "Come on, babe. Let's get you fed and drugged."

Growling under his breath, Duncan hated it when the other two noticed his problem. "Let's just eat." Purposefully, Duncan walked off in the direction of the kitchen, leaving the other two to follow.

Sighing quietly, Eezy grabbed for Chase's arm, keeping him back for a moment. "One of us needs to talk to him. Or at least bitch him out for his attitude."

"And start a fight," Chase added with a sigh. "The last time we tried, he railed and screamed and slept on the couch because he was so pissed off from staying in bed, remember?"

Eezy's brow furrowed in a deep frown. "No, not a fight. Not this time. If we have to, we'll tie him down and force him to listen. It's gone far enough. You set out the dinner, I'll tackle him."

Letting go of him, Eezy walked into the kitchen. The disturbed frown was still on his face as he eyed Duncan then sat down next to him.

Chase didn't say anything at first, just set the food on the table. When he walked back into the kitchen, he caught Eezy's glance from over the bar separating the kitchen and the dining room. "What do you two want to drink?"

"Water for me," Eezy said. "Duncan?"

"Water's fine." Still disgruntled, Duncan fingered his fork without looking up at the other two.

Eezy gritted his teeth, clearly resisting the urge to throttle Duncan. After taking a deep breath, he reached across the table, laying his hand on Duncan's. "You want what you want, and when we give it to you, you get all pissed off when we become concerned."

Finally, Duncan looked up at Eezy and was about to retort to the words before Eezy held up his hand. "This time you let me finish." There was a bang from one of the cabinets in the kitchen, followed by a low grumble. Eezy continued. "We sit by and watch you strain yourself every day. We hear the grunts and groans, we see when you hurt. We know you're going stir-crazy, but damn it, we want to make sure you're well before you manage anything worse."

When Duncan tried to stand, Eezy kept hold of his hand, forcing him to sit back down. "Flat out, Duncan. We both bend over backwards for you. Then you get pissed because we try to help when you do more than you should. If you aren't going to accept your limitations, then you better fucking well be ready to accept our help when you fucking need it."

Anger flared in Duncan's eyes briefly as he tried to free his hand. A moment later after Eezy's words sunk in, the anger deflated. Near to tears, he looked helplessly over at Chase.

Chase was still in the kitchen, but he was leaning forward against the bar. Three glasses of ice water sat in front of him. "Don't destroy yourself," he said quietly.

Finally, Eezy let go of his hand and Duncan reached for his fork to eat his dinner. He didn't say anything. Even though he knew Eezy was right, it didn't make it any easier to swallow.

Chapter Twenty-Seven

Duncan sat on the highest dune, overlooking the beach. The glow of the moons brought crystal clarity to the landscape, bathing it in a wash of silver. There was no sound but that of the sea and the few aquatic creatures nearby. Sifting the glittering blue sand through his fingers, he looked out over the water. He had a lot of things to think about, and the sound of the waves helped to relax him.

At times he became more frustrated than he could handle. Taking it this easy wasn't something he was used to. Yet if he overdid it, the pain meds he took would wear off more quickly. There had been quite a few times that he wouldn't have given a damn about that. He knew Chase and Eezy wanted to help him. If either of them were in this situation, he'd be doing the same thing they were.

Lately Duncan had been difficult, and he knew it. He really didn't mean to be, but there were times when Eezy and Chase drove him up a wall. He'd been surprised when neither had tried to stop him from coming to the beach, but Duncan just needed to cool off. Knowing better than to walk too far, he had only walked to the nearest rise to sit on the dune. This wasn't one of those times that he felt like overdoing it. If only he could get Chase and Eezy to understand.

Looking back over his shoulder at the house behind him, Duncan had to smile. He could see Eezy standing in the window, looking toward the beach. No doubt, he was trying to unobtrusively keep an eye on Duncan. Standing slowly, Duncan began walking back home.

The house was silent when he entered. Inside the front door, he paused to brush off the blue sand from his pants. Heading back to the kitchen, he opened the cupboard to get his medication out. He downed the pills with a drink of water then leaned against the cabinet, waiting for them to kick in.

"Hey." Eezy left the doorway and walked over to Duncan, hands sliding up Duncan's arms. "I..." He sighed and looked at a point over Duncan's shoulder. "I'm sorry."

As he closed his eyes, Duncan leaned in against him and laid his head on Eezy's shoulder. "I'm tired of the pills, I'm tired of the pain, and I'm tired of not being able to do what I want." Aware of how pathetic he sounded, Duncan sighed. "You don't need to apologize. I do."

"Look at me." Eezy's fingers slid through Duncan's hair, tilting his head up to meet Eezy's gaze. "We love you, Duncan. We don't want to watch you sink further into this. Healing takes time and effort. We're here for you always, but we can't make it go any faster. Only you can, by taking it easy and following the doctor's instructions."

"I know, I know. I owe both you and Chase an apology. Just sometimes, I want to do something, and it doesn't matter if I'm in pain or not. I can deal with that. Do you understand what I mean?" Locking his gaze with Eezy, he begged his lover to understand.

Eezy sighed. "I do, love. I do." He smiled a little and stroked his fingers down the side of Duncan's face. "Maybe we can compromise. Work out what you can and can't handle. But you have to promise not to push yourself, to let us help you when you honestly need it, instead of shoving us away."

"I think I can handle both of you every once in a while and not get too pissed when you try to help me afterwards." A small grin appeared on Duncan's lips. "We should find Chase. I need to talk to him, too."

"I'll leave you to that." Eezy smiled and kissed him softly. "I think he went to get a shower."

Duncan bit gently at Eezy's lip then released him, nodding. "Yeah, I'll take care of it."

Untangling himself, Duncan left the kitchen and walked down the back hall towards the bathroom. He had every intention of joining his husband in the shower and as he undressed, he left a trail of clothes behind him. Silently, he opened the bathroom door and stepped inside. He could see the outline of Chase's body through the frosted glass of the shower door. Instantly Duncan could feel Chase's lost mood, seeing him leaning against the tile of the shower.

Without saying anything, Duncan opened the shower door and stepped in behind Chase, then slid his arms around him, hugging tightly.

One of Chase's hands covered his, but the captain didn't move otherwise. His fingers tightened around Duncan's and Chase let out a long breath. "Miss you," he said quietly, barely audible over the constant drum of water around them.

"I'm sorry, love." Pressing a kiss to Chase's shoulder, Duncan tasted him as he held Chase. "I've been a bastard to both you and Eezy. And I'm really sorry."

"Don't be." Chase turned in his arms and pulled Duncan close. "Just know that we do it because we love you more than life itself."

"That's something neither of you need to tell me." Meeting Chase's eyes, Duncan gave him a rueful smile. "Sometimes I want to do things no matter how much it hurts later. And right now, you're one of them."

Before Chase could protest, Duncan silenced him with a hard kiss. The hungry probe of his tongue slipped between Chase's lips, wanting the warmth within.

Chase's surprised gasp filled the kiss. His arms draped over Duncan's shoulders and soon he was all but melting, body flush with Duncan's. "Please," he whispered on Duncan's lips. "I need you."

His lips recaptured Chase's. They both needed each other, and Duncan planned on showing Chase just how much he was loved. Both hands tenderly caressed over the wetness of Chase's chest as Duncan pressed him back against the tile.

"Bed." Chase reached down and turned off the water. "I need to feel you, Duncan. Everywhere."

Duncan didn't care where they were. He reached for the towel and started drying Chase off. The whole time Duncan's eyes never left him. "I know what you need, love. Why do you think I'm so determined to give it to you?"

The painkillers were doing the job of keeping any pain at bay, though Duncan knew the exertion would make them wear off faster. Not something he cared about either; and this time he would let Eezy and Chase take care of him afterwards.

Once they were dry, Duncan pulled Chase with him out of the bathroom and into the bedroom.

Chase crawled onto the bed, pulling Duncan gently down with him. He didn't say anything, just reached over to the bedside table and got the lube. Setting it on the bed beside them, he circled Duncan's neck with his arms, pulling Duncan down for another deep kiss.

Not in the mood to hurry, Duncan took his sweet time tasting Chase's mouth. His tongue ran slowly beneath the edge of his teeth, tantalizing Chase, then slid deeper, circling slowly. When he finally drew back, he dipped his head and lavished more kisses and licks over Chase's chest, stopping only to nip lightly at his nipple, tugging it gently with his teeth. He loved the taste and feel of Chase and savored the long moment of getting his fill.

A soft hiss of breath met him, Chase's fingers tunneling through Duncan's hair. Chase parted his legs and he shifted until Duncan was between them, bracketed by Chase's thighs. Tilting his head back, Chase moaned softly, hands kneading down over Duncan's shoulders, not pushing, simply feeling.

Sometimes Duncan felt so much that he didn't have the words. The only thing he could do was worship the ones he loved. Each breath left a cooling sensation in the wake of his kisses as he covered every inch of Chase's chest. The tip of his tongue trailed over the rise of muscle, moving downward to dip teasingly into his belly button. His fingers ran along the top of Chase's thigh then edged back up in a light touch, feeling every one of Chase's reactions.

"Want you, babe. Not sure how long I can hold out."

"Don't wait." Chase rose up onto his elbows and looked down at Duncan. "This isn't about sex, Duncan. It's about us: reconnecting, reaffirming."

Smiling up at him, Duncan knew exactly what they were doing. Shifting, he slid slowly over Chase's body until their faces were level then pressed a soft kiss to Chase's lips. "This is to show you how much I do love you."

Chase nodded and wrapped his legs around Duncan's waist, urging him closer. "Love you, too," he whispered.

The bed dipped beside them and Eezy smoothed his hand over Duncan's back. "Don't move."

Smiling, Chase lifted his head for a kiss. Just as Duncan's tongue slipped into his mouth, Chase moaned deeply, hips rocking as Eezy's slick fingers pushed inside him. Then they were gone and without breaking the kiss, Duncan shifted and slid inside him. The movements were slow and deep, every one taking Chase's breath away.

Lifting his head, Duncan watched as Eezy leaned in, capturing Chase's lips in another kiss. Eezy's hand slid between them and began pumping Chase's cock. The slow rhythm of Duncan's body repeatedly took him as Chase writhed between the hand and cock.

Eezy broke the kiss, and Duncan nuzzled Chase's neck, the navigator's thrusts growing in strength, his moans rolling through Chase.

Looking up, Chase stared at Eezy, then tumbled over the edge, shuddering out his release. The erotic display held Eezy spellbound.

"Chase..." Duncan bit down on Chase's shoulder and cried out, cock pulsing deep inside him.

Taking several breaths, Duncan lifted his head and gazed down at Chase. "I promise not to get so upset over everything anymore. Just have patience with me as well."

"Don't you know I'd do anything for you, love? For both of you." Chase's expression softened as he studied them.

"So beautiful," Eezy murmured, kissing Duncan's shoulder. He smiled when he met Chase's gaze again, the love between the three of them tangible. "My beautiful men."

ABOUT THE AUTHORS

Mychael Black
Alter ego of Katherine Cook, Mychael focuses on gay erotic romance stories in many genres. He lives in the eastern US with his family.
https://www.mychaelblack.com
https://www.facebook.com/mblackauthor/

Shayne Carmichael
She writes, she makes shiny things.